UPTON UNDERTAKERS

A captivating Victorian historical murder mystery

KERRY TOMBS

Inspector Ravenscroft Detective Mysteries Book 7

JOFFE BOOKS

Revised edition 2020
Joffe Books, London
www.joffebooks.com

First published in Great Britain 2015

ISBN 978-1-78931-563-9

To Joan, Zoe and Samuel
Happy memories of Upton and Malvern

PROLOGUE

MATHON CHURCHYARD, MARCH 1891

He had always disliked funerals.

Whether it was the occasion itself with its degrees of solemnity and finality, or the fact that he would have to converse with comparative strangers, he could not be sure, but he knew that such gatherings had usually been accompanied by cold and rain, and as he stepped down from the carriage and looked up at the threatening sky above, Anthony knew that today would prove no exception to the rule. Only the subject of this burial afforded a change from the expected. The white card with its black edging, which he had received the previous day, had informed him of the sudden demise of Simon Cleaves — dead as the result of a fall from his horse — a young gentleman of some twenty-five years or so.

'Where shall I wait for you, Mr Midwinter?' enquired the cabman.

'Down the road if you will,' replied Anthony, giving the man a coin. 'I trust that the event will not be of a protracted duration.'

'As you wish, sir. Come along there, boy,' replied the man, cracking his whip.

Anthony opened the creaking gate of the churchyard and made his slow way towards the group of figures clustered around the main entrance to the church, pausing only to glance at the open grave, and remembering the time when he had attended the funerals of Simon's parents, Martin and Janet Cleaves. They had each died within six months of each other, some ten or eleven years previously, and Anthony observed that the inscription on their stone was already beginning to show signs of wear.

He had been attending such services for over forty years, since he had joined the legal practice in Ledbury as an articled pupil, and recalled that only five years had then passed when old Burrow's son had died unexpectedly, and he had used what little money he had inherited to buy into the firm. Then, shortly afterwards, Burrows himself had been called to his Maker, and Anthony had found himself the senior, and sole, partner. Shortly afterwards he had married, but two years later he had buried what was to be his only child, and since then it had seemed that the many long empty years had followed without hope or purpose, years in which he had slowly witnessed the demise of the firm's oldest clients, one after another, as he himself had grown older.

As he drew nearer to the porch he could hear voices.

'What a great tragedy this is, my dear. Simon was so young. He should not have died like this,' said the elder of the two speakers.

'Do not distress yourself, Aunt. We must be brave,' replied the other.

'It only seemed like yesterday that you and your brother came to stay with me at Fordlands. I can see you now, playing on the lawn; Simon's mischievous smile, your beautiful flowing locks, and both of you laughing as you both tried to play croquet with those large mallets.'

'That is what we must do, Aunt: remember Simon as he would have wanted us to remember him.'

'Yes, my dear; but it is hard.'

Anthony, considering the time opportune to pay his respects, stepped forward, and, removing his hat, addressed the two women. 'Lady Cleaves, Miss Anne, may I be so bold as to express my condolences, on behalf of Midwinter, Oliphant and Burrows, for your sad and sudden loss?'

'That is most kind of you, Mr Midwinter. I am pleased that you were able to attend,' replied Lady Cleaves from beneath her veil.

'I think we might begin, Your Ladyship,' said the vicar, emerging from within the church.

Anthony stood to one side, as the two women linked arms and made their way out of the building and along the path towards the open grave, followed by a number of other people whom he assumed to be the family servants. Arriving at the graveside he gave a short nod of recognition in the direction of the three black-suited undertakers who stood by the side of the coffin. Shortcross and Maudlin of Upton had conducted so many of the funerals he had attended over the years.

'Gentlemen, if you would lower the coffin to its resting place,' instructed the clergyman.

'Take hold of the rope, Brothers,' said one of the three men stepping forward.

'Pray be gentle with my nephew,' instructed Lady Cleaves.

'Rest assured, Your Ladyship,' replied the undertaker. 'Lower him slowly, Brothers.'

'We are gathered here today to witness the burial of Simon Cleaves, late of Mathon Manor . . .' began the vicar.

Anthony turned away as the coffin was lowered into the ground, and observed a tall, black-coated figure, standing some way off at the other side of the churchyard, and wondered why this man had not joined the other mourners. Drops of rain began to fall on the wood of the coffin, and the cold wind that blew seemed only to increase his personal discomfort and unease.

'—we therefore commit his body to the ground; earth to earth, ashes to ashes, dust to dust; in sure and certain hope of the Resurrection to Eternal Life.'

A sobbing Ann Cleaves stepped forward and threw a small bouquet of flowers onto the coffin.

'Stop! You cannot proceed with this burial.'

Anthony looked up and saw that the intervention had come from the old lady.

'Lady Cleaves?' enquired the startled vicar.

'Did you not hear that sound?'

'What sound, Your Ladyship?'

'I heard a sound from within the coffin. My nephew — he must be alive!'

'I heard nothing,' said one of the undertakers giving a puzzled look in the direction of his two companions.

'I tell you I heard a sound from within the casket. You must have heard it as well, Anne?' continued Lady Cleaves.

'I think you must be mistaken, Aunt. I did not hear anything,' answered her niece, seeking to placate the old lady.

'Mr Midwinter, will you not tell them that you heard the sound?' pleaded Lady Cleaves turning in Anthony's direction.

'I . . . I must confess, ma'am, that I did not hear anything,' stuttered Anthony becoming uneasy with this interruption in the service, and wondering what would happen next.

'I tell you I heard strange sounds from within the coffin. Why did no one else hear them?' protested Lady Cleaves, becoming more and more agitated as she looked at all around her.

'Come away, Aunt; let us wait in the carriage,' suggested Anne.

'No. I tell you I heard noises. Poor Simon must be alive. You must open it.'

'This is highly irregular,' protested the clergyman.

'I tell you, bring up the coffin,' said Lady Cleaves raising her voice. 'Here, you men, you must bring up the coffin, I say!'

'There's nothing else for it, Brothers,' said the chief undertaker reluctantly. 'Brother Benjamin, and Brother Simeon, if you would be so kind.'

The two undertakers gave each other a strange look, before climbing into the grave, where they secured the ropes around the coffin.

'Now, Brothers, lift if you will,' instructed their associate.

Anthony turned away as the coffin was raised to the ground, and wished that he was anywhere else but in Mathon churchyard.

'Undo the screws, Brothers,' ordered the undertaker.

The small congregation edged slowly nearer as the coffin lid was slowly removed. Anthony bought out his handkerchief to his nose and felt a chill run down his spine. Someone in the background let out a muffled scream.

'Well, he looks dead enough to me,' remarked one of the onlookers.

'I can assure Your Ladyship that he was dead when we placed him in the coffin yesterday evening,' offered the chief undertaker. 'Was he not, Brothers?'

'Indeed so, Brother,' confirmed one of the others.

'But that man is not my nephew!' exclaimed Lady Cleaves staring into the coffin. 'That is not Simon. Tell them, Anne, that this man is not your brother.'

'You are right, Aunt. There has been some terrible mistake,' said Anne Cleaves, her voice trembling with emotion.

'Mansfield, will you tell them all that this man is not your master?' continued Lady Cleaves beckoning to one of the servants.

'This man is not Mr Simon Cleaves,' replied the tall grey-haired man.

'Where is my nephew? What have you done with my nephew?' shouted Lady Cleaves addressing the three startled undertakers.

'I can assure Your Ladyship that this is the man we placed in the casket last night. We were under the impression that the deceased gentleman was Mr Simon Cleaves,' replied the chief undertaker, a look of fear and anxiety spreading across his face.

'So this man is not Mr Simon Cleaves?' said the vicar. 'Then who is he?'

'I have never seen this man before,' announced an indignant Lady Cleaves.

'He is the man we put in the coffin, is he not, Brothers?' repeated the undertaker.

'That he is, Brother Reuben,' answered each of the other two men in turn.

'Anne, do you see what this means? Simon must still be alive,' pronounced Lady Cleaves. 'My nephew is still alive!'

'Forgive me, Lady Cleaves, Miss Cleaves; if you both insist that this man is not your relative, I am afraid I must decline to conclude this service,' protested the vicar. 'Does anyone here know who this man is?'

Various members of the congregation edged forward; several shook their heads, while others briefly stared into the coffin before turning away with puzzled expressions on their faces. Anthony looked across the churchyard and observed that the black-coated onlooker was walking quickly away from the scene.

'Dear me, what are we to do now?' asked Lady Cleaves. 'This has all been most unsettling. Perhaps you can be of assistance to us in this matter, Mr Midwinter?'

'Er . . . well . . . yes,' began a startled Anthony, unsettled that he had been suddenly thrown into the limelight, and conscious that all eyes were now upon him to offer some solution to help resolve the situation. 'Well, yes, I think it would be best if the unfortunate corpse is removed to your premises in Upton, Mr Thexton, and that we inform the appropriate authorities.'

'Very well, Mr Midwinter. That would seem to be an excellent suggestion, if I may say. My niece and I will return home,' pronounced Lady Cleaves, beginning to take her leave.

'Well, this is a peculiar state of affairs, and no mistake,' muttered one of the undertakers.

‘It is indeed, Mr Thexton,’ said Brother Benjamin shaking his head

‘Perhaps, Mr Midwinter, you might also be able to instruct someone to find the real whereabouts of my nephew?’ said Lady Cleaves.

‘Certainly, Lady Cleaves. I might just know of a man who can help us solve this strange difficulty,’ replied Anthony. ‘Yes, indeed.’

CHAPTER ONE

LEDBURY AND UPTON-UPON-SEVERN

'Good heavens!' exclaimed Lucy.

Ravenscroft lowered his newspaper and peered at his wife over the top of his spectacles.

'How absolutely terrible!' continued Lucy.

'What is?'

'It says here in this book that when William Burke, the notorious body snatcher, was executed, souvenir hunters fought amongst themselves to secure pieces of wood from his coffin, and that when his body was publicly dissected the following day, crowds flocked to view his corpse, after the surgeon had taken out his brain!'

'Served him right, I say, for killing all those people, and selling their bodies to the medical men,' said Ravenscroft. 'In my opinion the man got what he deserved.'

The detective and his wife were sitting before an open fire in their small cottage, in the Herefordshire market town of Ledbury.

'There is even a wallet made from Burke's scalp on display in Edinburgh's Royal College of Surgeons!'

'Looks as though your book is quite interesting, my dear,' smiled Ravenscroft.

'Well, all I can say is that it's a good thing that we don't have public executions in this country anymore.'

'Yes, I think that was stopped in 1868.'

'They both sound quite horrible, Burke and his partner Hare; killing all those innocent people, and then digging up their bodies, after they had been buried, so that they could then sell them.'

'They were called resurrection men, I believe. Their victims were mainly elderly, frail people without any relatives or friends, so they were not missed when Burke and Hare poisoned them.'

'Thank goodness that sort of thing does not happen today. Apparently this book also says that one old woman had such a fear of being buried alive by mistake, that she gave instructions before she passed away, that one end of a piece of string should be tied to one of her fingers, and the other end tied to small bell at the side of the burial plot, so that if she awoke and found herself inside the coffin she could pull the string, and the bell would then ring, and she would be saved.'

'And did this plan work?' asked Ravenscroft, curiously.

'Well, shortly after the poor woman died and had been duly buried, the following night the bell rang quite violently, and all the village people rushed out of their homes, but when they raised the coffin they found that the old woman was quite dead. Apparently it had been the wind that had caused the bell to ring.'

'Must have given her relatives a fright,' said Ravenscroft throwing another log on the fire, before resuming the reading of his newspaper.

'Samuel, there is something which I need to talk to you about,' said Lucy laying her book aside after a few minutes had elapsed.

Ravenscroft, recognizing the serious tone of his wife's voice, folded his paper neatly onto his lap.

'I am very worried about young Richard.'

'Why? I hope he is not ill?'

'No, he is quite well, but I'm afraid he came home from school today in quite an agitated state. He was very upset and crying. And this was not the first time. He came home very distressed twice last week.'

'Have you asked what ails him?'

'Yes. It seems that he is being bullied quite a great deal at school. The main offenders seem to be those terrible Leewood children and their friends.'

'I see. I will go and have a word with the headmistress tomorrow morning.'

'With all due respect, I only think that would make matters worse. The children know that Richard's father is a policeman, and they are inclined to take it out on him.'

'I suppose it does not help that I have put away several of their fathers over the past two years. I appreciate it must be hard for him.'

'So, I was wondering if it might be better if Richard were sent away to a boarding school, away from Ledbury, where the children would not know that his father is a policeman. I know he is only six, but lots of children of his age are sent away to such establishments these days. I have a little money put by since Uncle George died last year, and your salary could help.'

'You would miss him frightfully,' suggested Ravenscroft.

'Of course, but we still have little Arthur, and Richard would be home for the holidays and perhaps even some weekends. I am sure he would benefit so,' continued his wife, warming to her subject.

'Yes, I see all that, but where would we find such a suitable school?'

'On the back page of your paper,' answered Lucy smiling.

Ravenscroft reopened the folded newspaper and turned to the back page. 'Yes here we are: Carter's Little Liver Pills. No, it cannot be that. "Colwall Cricket Team Prepare for the New Season."'

'Stop teasing, Samuel. I know that you can see the advertisement quite well at the bottom of the third column,' reprimanded Lucy.

'Ah yes. "Glenforest Preparatory School is situated on the Downs, near the Herefordshire market town of Bromyard. Boys are taken from five years upwards and educated to the highest standards. Latin, English, History and Mathematics are our specialities. Healthy sports are undertaken by all pupils. Please contact the Principal, Mr Horace Smeaton MA, for further details." It sounds quite promising. Perhaps we should make an appointment?'

'I already have!' announced Lucy. 'I have contacted Mr Smeaton and he has agreed to see us on Wednesday morning at eleven o'clock.'

'Well, I see you have been quite busy on our behalf.'

'You don't mind, do you? You don't seem to be very busy at the moment, so I thought it would do no harm to arrange things.'

'I would have expected nothing else from you, my dear.'

'Good. Then that is settled. I know it might not be suitable, but unless we go and visit we shall never know.'

'I quite agree. You did the right thing.'

'Sorry to intrude, Mr Ravenscroft, Mrs Ravenscroft, but there is a gentleman who requests an urgent word with you, sir,' interrupted the maid.

'Did you not instruct him to proceed to the police station?' asked Ravenscroft.

'I did, sir, but he seems quite agitated and says that it is imperative that he sees you straight away. I think it is Mr Midwinter, the solicitor, if I am not mistaken,' she continued.

'Mr Midwinter you say? Then you had better show him in at once.'

'Thank you, my good sir,' said the distressed solicitor rushing into the room. 'Please excuse the intrusion, Mrs Ravenscroft, but I would have not disturbed your husband so if the matter had not been of the gravest importance.'

'Please do take a seat, Mr Midwinter. It is good to see you again,' replied Ravenscroft.

'Thank you, my dear sir,' said Midwinter, accepting the chair and bringing out a handkerchief to mop his perspiring brow.

'Perhaps you would care for some tea, Mr Midwinter?' asked Lucy.

'No, thank you, Mrs Ravenscroft. You must excuse my being somewhat out of breath. I came as quickly as I could. It is all a terrible state of affairs I can assure you. They nearly buried the wrong man!'

'Dear me,' said Lucy, hastily covering over her reading book with her husband's newspaper.

'Please take your time, Mr Midwinter,' suggested Ravenscroft.

'Yes, indeed so.'

During the next few minutes the solicitor narrated the events of earlier that day.

'What an extraordinary state of affairs!' exclaimed Lucy, once Midwinter had concluded his story.

'Indeed. And you say that the body of this unknown man has now been removed to the undertakers in Upton-upon-Severn?' asked Ravenscroft.

'Yes, Mr Ravenscroft.'

'And what has happened to Lady Cleaves and her niece?'

'They have returned to Mathon Manor. I told them to expect a visit from your good self.'

'Thank you; and you say that no one knows who the dead person is?'

'It would appear so.'

'This is a strange affair indeed. You have acted quite correctly, Mr Midwinter, in bringing this matter to my attention. I can assure you that my associate, Mr Crabb, and I will travel over to Upton without delay.'

'I must say that is something of a relief.'

'Rest assured, Mr Midwinter, that we will soon get to the truth of this matter. I am sure that there is a quite logical explanation for all this.'

'Would you like me to accompany you, Inspector?'

'That will not be necessary, sir, but of course, I will keep you fully informed of developments.'

* * *

The last remnants of daylight were beginning to fade as Ravenscroft and Crabb entered the small Worcestershire market town of Upton-upon-Severn, passing along the main street with its unprepossessing shops and houses, until they found themselves drawing closer to the riverbank, where the majestic clock tower surmounted by its fine cupola stood tall over the old churchyard and nearby inns. A few more yards bought them to the outside of a small cottage which Ravenscroft knew served as the local police station.

'Tie the horse up over there, Tom,' instructed Ravenscroft, as he alighted from the trap.

'There appears to be no one here, sir,' said Crabb as the two detectives entered the front room of the building.

'Anyone about?' shouted Ravenscroft, banging on the counter after a few moments had elapsed.

'All right, all right, I'm coming,' replied a stout, red-faced policeman emerging from the inner room, holding a large tart in one hand, while hastily doing up the buttons of his tunic with the other.

'Good lord, Hoskings!' exclaimed Ravenscroft. 'What the deuce are you doing here? Where is Inspector Checketts?'

'Away on leave, sir,' replied the embarrassed policeman after quickly swallowing, and seeking to dispose of the remains of his tart beneath the counter.

'I thought you served in the station at Pershore?' asked Ravenscroft.

'I was — I mean, I am sir, but they sent me here a few days ago to look after the station while the inspector is away,' answered the constable growing even redder in the face as he quickly brushed away some crumbs that had fallen down the front of his tunic.

'Well, I suppose you will have to do,' Ravenscroft sighed. 'Now what can you tell us about this dead man?'

'What dead man sir?'

'The dead man who was almost buried in mistake for Mr Simon Cleaves.'

'Oh yes, sir, that dead man, of course, sir.'

'Well, man, get on with it. We have not got all day,' instructed an impatient Ravenscroft.

'Yes, sir, of course, sir,' replied the constable, removing his pocket book from the top pocket of his tunic and beginning to read from the opened page. 'On Saturday afternoon at precisely four-thirty I was called to the meadow, by the banks of the river, where I found a deceased person lying on the ground. When I examined the body I concluded that the deceased person had died of wounds sustained as the result of a fall from his horse —'

'Just one moment, Hoskings,' interrupted Ravenscroft. 'How did you know that the deceased had died as the result of a fall from his horse?'

'There was blood at the top and back of his head, sir, and there was a horse in the same field.'

'Was the horse saddled?'

'It was, sir.'

'What did you do next?'

'I immediately sent a messenger to summon a doctor. Doctor Stapleford arrived shortly afterwards and examined the body and confirmed that the deceased gentleman was in fact . . . er . . . well . . . er . . . deceased.'

'How did you establish the identity of this man?'

'An examination of the gentleman's pockets revealed a fob watch inscribed with the letters S.C. on the reverse, and a leather wallet containing a number of personal papers which gave his name as a Mr Simon Cleaves of Mathon Manor.'

'What did you do next, Hoskings?'

'I sent word to Mr Thexton of Shortcross and Maudlin Undertakers, and they arrived soon afterwards and removed the body to their premises in Court Street.'

'And how did you inform Mr Cleaves's family of his demise?' questioned Ravenscroft.

'I journeyed over to Mathon Court, taking the horse and one of the stable lads from the White Lion with me. They were able to confirm that the horse belonged to Mr Cleaves, as well as identifying the wallet and watch.'

'And where is this wallet and watch now?'

'I gave them to Miss Cleaves, sir.'

'You gave them to Miss Cleaves!' exclaimed Ravenscroft. 'They should have been retained as evidence.'

'Yes, sir. Sorry, sir. It was just that Miss Cleaves asked if she could keep her brother's effects, and I could see no problem with it, sir.'

'Good grief, man, don't you know the first rule of policing? You always retain the evidence,' interjected Ravenscroft.

'Yes, sir. Sorry, sir,' repeated a crestfallen Hoskings.

'Did you ask Miss Cleaves to return with you to identify the dead man as her brother?'

'No, sir.'

'Why ever not, man?'

'Miss Cleaves was very distressed by my news, sir.'

'And it did not occur to you to insist that someone else from the house might have returned with you?'

'No, sir.'

'Hoskings, this is a disgraceful state of affairs. You should have known the importance of obtaining a positive identification from either relatives or close friends. It is thanks to you that the wrong man was nearly buried today,' glared Ravenscroft.

'Sorry, sir,' muttered the policeman, looking down at his boots sheepishly.

'Where are these undertakers to be found?' asked Ravenscroft.

'They are in Court Street, sir, just off Old Street. About halfway down on the left-hand side. There is a sign outside.'

'Constable Crabb and I will go and view the body. Is there a photographer in the town?'

'Yes, sir, but why do you need a photographer?' asked Hoskings, looking perplexed.

'We need him so that we can obtain some photographs of the dead man. Quite clearly he is not Mr Simon Cleaves and, as no one seems to know who he is, we will need images of the man to try and establish his identity. I would have thought that was obvious.'

'Yes, sir.'

'Well, don't just stand there, man. Go and find this photographer and tell him to bring his equipment as soon as possible to Shortcross and Maudlin.'

'Yes, sir.'

'And, Hoskings, do up the buttons on your tunic in the correct order, before you leave the office.'

'Yes, sir. Sorry, sir.'

* * *

A few minutes later Ravenscroft and Crabb found themselves standing outside a large doubled-fronted wooden building in one of the narrow streets of the town, where the words 'Shortcross and Maudlin' were badly painted on a cracked hanging sign that was creaking back and forth in the night air.

'Looks like a coat of paint would not go amiss,' remarked Crabb, as Ravenscroft pushed open the door.

The two men found themselves standing in what appeared to be a large yard, where the smell of horse manure hung in the air, and an old dangling gas lamp spluttered forth an intermittent blue flame. Ravenscroft picked his way across the dark yard with care until he reached the building at the rear.

'Yes?' enquired a figure, suddenly opening a door and holding up an oil lamp in one hand.

'I presume I have the honour of addressing Mr Maudlin?' asked Ravenscroft.

'Mr Maudlin has been dead these past forty years,' replied the man gloomily.

'Oh, I am sorry to hear that. You must be Mr Shortcross then?' smiled Ravenscroft, observing that the undertaker possessed a nose that was too large for his long haggard face, and that he was being stared at through large, piercing eyes.

'Alas no, Mr Shortcross left us thirty years ago.'

'Deceased as well?'

'No, sir. Alive and well in Eastbourne I believe — with Mrs Maudlin.'

'I see. So you are?'

'Thexton, sir, Mr Reuben Thexton at your service. How may I be of assistance? A loving parent has departed this world perhaps? No? A maiden aunt unexpectedly passed away? An aged grandparent carried away to Abraham's breast? No? It must be an esteemed friend then, or possibly an ancient uncle?' asked the undertaker with great solemnity as he rubbed his hands together gently.

'No, it is none of those. We have no need of your professional services, I can assure you. We are the police. My name is Detective Inspector Ravenscroft and this is my associate, Constable Crabb.'

'Ah, you have no doubt come to enquire about the gentleman who was nearly buried today.'

'Indeed so. I would be obliged if you would answer some questions.'

'You had better enter then, gentlemen,' replied Thexton, stepping to one side of the entrance to allow Ravenscroft and Crabb to enter into a gloomy, musty-smelling room.

'Who is it, Brother Reuben?' called out a voice from within the darkness.

'Gentlemen from the police enquiring about the deceased,' answered the undertaker.

'Detective Inspector Ravenscroft and Constable Crabb,' said Ravenscroft, straining to see the outlines of two other figures at the back of the room.

'This is a terrible state of affairs,' said one of the men drawing nearer.

'Terrible, Brother Benjamin,' added another holding a candle aloft.

'Perhaps you would be kind enough to tell us your part in this matter?' asked Ravenscroft, observing that, as the other two men drew nearer they seemed to strongly resemble the first speaker in appearance.

'Your constable sent for us to collect the body from near the river,' answered Reuben.

'Which we did, did we not, Simeon?' added Benjamin.

'We did indeed, Brother Benjamin,' emphasized the third brother staring hard at Crabb.

'Can you tell us how you established the identity of the said gentleman?' asked Ravenscroft, amused by the trio of answers.

'That was your constable. I believe he found some items in the pockets of the dead man which suggested that he was a Mr Simon Cleaves of Mathon,' replied Reuben, giving a kind of half smile that Ravenscroft found unsettling.

'A Mr Simon Cleaves of Mathon,' added Benjamin.

'Cleaves of Mathon,' muttered Simeon.

'Had either of you ever previously seen Mr Cleaves?' asked Crabb.

'No, the gentleman was not known to us,' pronounced Reuben.

'Not known indeed.'

'He was completely unknown to us, my dear sir; never seen before.'

'And can you all confirm that the dead man you collected on Saturday was the same man that you took to Mathon churchyard to be buried earlier today?' asked Ravenscroft.

'That was indeed so.'

'Identical.'

'He was one and the same.'

'Was the body at any time left unattended during its time on your premises?' enquired Ravenscroft, anxious to know more.

'Oh no, once a body arrives here we always make sure that one of us remains with the dearly departed until the time of burial,' answered Reuben in a serious tone of voice as he bowed his head.

'I would be obliged if we could examine the body,' requested Ravenscroft.

Reuben looked at his two brothers anxiously.

'It is important that we do so,' emphasized Ravenscroft.

'Then you had better enter our inner sanctum,' replied Reuben, reluctantly holding the oil lamp aloft and indicating that the policemen were to follow him.

Ravenscroft and Crabb now found themselves entering a smaller, even darker room, the floor of which seemed to be covered with wood chippings and sawdust, and where the stale air seemed pungent with the aromas of damp, decay and death.

'You will find the deceased still there inside the coffin,' said Reuben nervously.

Ravenscroft and Crabb edged slowly forwards, towards the trestle table in the centre of the room, upon which lay an open coffin.

'I would be grateful if you could bring the lamp nearer so that I can see the body, Mr Thexton,' requested Ravenscroft removing his handkerchief from his coat pocket and bringing it towards his nose.

The undertaker held the lamp high above the coffin. Ravenscroft looked down at the yellowing pallid face of the dead man, before cautiously bending forwards and raising the head of the deceased and examining the damaged area at the back of the skull.

'What age would you say the man was, Constable?'

'I would say that he was in his middle twenties, sir,' said Crabb, inching nearer while at the same time being determined to keep his distance.

'That was what I concluded,' agreed Ravenscroft lifting up the dead man's hands and examining the fingers. 'I take it there is nothing remaining in the dead man's pockets, gentlemen?'

'No, sir,' replied Reuben Thexton.

'Your constable made a detailed search,' said Benjamin, drawing closer to the coffin so that the light from his candle flickered across his face, giving it an almost ghostly appearance.

'Completely empty,' added Simeon Thexton somewhere in the darkness.

'I presume that the deceased is still wearing the same attire in which he was found,' said Ravenscroft, running his hands inside the pockets of the dead man's clothes.

'Indeed so, Inspector,' replied Reuben.

'We never change a deceased's clothing,'

'Never; it would be a violation.'

'Thank you, gentlemen, you have all been most helpful. I have taken the liberty of engaging a local photographer who should be with you shortly. As we are unaware of this gentleman's identity we must circulate photographs in the hope that someone may be able to identify him. I would be obliged if you would instruct the man to take six photographs of the deceased, including a close image of his face, and then indicate that they are to be delivered to the police station here in Upton before eight in the morning. I trust I have made myself clear on that point?' said Ravenscroft, anxious to leave the claustrophobic room as soon as possible.

'I will see that is carried out, Inspector,' said Reuben, giving again the same sickly smile that Ravenscroft had earlier found so disturbing.

'Good. Now can you inform us where this Dr Stapleford resides? We understand that it was this gentleman who examined the body,' continued Ravenscroft before the other two brothers could speak.

'If you would care to take the road towards Little Malvern, and travel for nearly half a mile from the town, up the hill, past the road to Gloucester, and then turn left, you will find a large white house at the bottom of the lane,' answered Reuben, in a dry factual tone of voice.

'I am obliged to you,' said Ravenscroft walking quickly back into the outer room. 'Good evening to you all.'

'And may the good Lord always be with you both,' said Benjamin his eyes looking towards the ceiling.

'Amen,' echoed Simeon.

'But pray, sir, what are we to do with this deceased gentleman?' asked a concerned Benjamin Thexton.

'Well, Mr Thexton, we cannot bury the deceased until we have established his identity, so I am afraid you must keep the body here until you receive further instructions,' said Ravenscroft, disappearing from view.

'But, but . . .' protested Reuben.

'What a terrible state of affairs,' muttered Simeon Thexton throwing up his arms in the air.

'Really, Brothers, this will not do at all, not at all,' added Benjamin.

* * *

'Well, Tom, what do you make of our three undertakers?' asked Ravenscroft as he climbed into the trap.

'They seemed identical to one another; it was difficult to tell them apart,' answered Crabb, urging the horse forward.

'Yes, but I think Reuben is evidently the eldest. I found it rather annoying that when one of them had spoken, the other two felt obliged to confirm what the other had said.'

'The whole undertaking was rather creepy if you ask me. I was glad when we got out of that room. The place gave me the shivers.'

'Their parents were evidently quite religious.'

'Oh, why do you say that, sir?'

'Reuben, Benjamin and Simeon are the names of three of the tribes of Israel. Rather appropriate for a trio of undertakers, I suppose. However, I got the distinct feeling that the brothers were not telling us everything they knew. They were certainly reluctant to let us view the corpse. What did you ascertain about the body?'

'The man was aged about twenty to thirty, not used to manual work by his hands and appearance,' said Crabb.

'Good.'

'He looked as though he had died as the result of a fall.'

'Yes, there was certainly extensive bruising at the back of the head, although there is no way of telling whether he sustained his injuries as the result of a fall, or whether he was struck by an attacker. However, in my experience, people generally fall forward rather than backward when they are thrown by a horse. Did you observe anything else about the man?'

'That waistcoat seemed rather too large for him.'

'Excellent. Was there anything else you noticed?'

'No, sir.'

'There was something I found in one of the trouser pockets, which had evidently been overlooked. I did not want to alert the Thexton brothers to my discovery,' said Ravenscroft, handing over the item to Crabb.

'A piece of chalk, sir!' exclaimed Crabb.

'Exactly, what kind of man carries a piece of chalk around with him in the pocket of his trousers?'

'A schoolteacher maybe, or a man who works in some kind of warehouse where he chalks numbers on the sides of crates.'

'Precisely! I also found ink stains on two of his fingers on the left hand, which would tend to support our theory.'

'So the dead man was a left-handed schoolteacher or clerk?'

'So it would seem. All we need to do now is to find either which educational establishment he taught in, or in which premises he worked as a clerk.'

'Not easy, sir. There must be thousands of schools and warehouses in the country.'

'Yes, but if we have photographs of the deceased by tomorrow, we can post a description in the local newspapers, as well as sending a copy to our main station in Worcester. I have no doubt then that someone will come forward and tell us who he is. What I find most interesting, however, is that if the dead man was in fact killed, his murderer must have been intent on planting Simon Cleaves's wallet and watch on his person, while at the same time removing anything from his victim's pockets that could have revealed his true identity.'

'Except for the chalk,' replied Crabb.

'Exactly.'

They had now left the lights of the town behind them and, as the trap made its way up the hill, Ravenscroft peered through the darkness seeking the turn that would eventually take them to Stapleford's residence.

'There, sir!' shouted Crabb, swinging the vehicle sharply to the left.

'I can see a light in the distance down the bottom of the lane,' said Ravenscroft.

The cab made its way down the bumpy, unkempt road and eventually came to a halt outside a large, imposing Georgian house.

'This must be where Dr Stapleford lives,' said Ravenscroft, jumping down from the trap. 'Tie up the horse to that post over there, Tom.'

Ravenscroft walked up the steps and tugged at the bell pull at the side of the door.

'Residents not at home?' suggested Crabb after some moments had elapsed.

'I don't think so. I thought I detected a noise from somewhere within,' said Ravenscroft, repeating his action.

Presently the sound of bolts being drawn back could be heard, before the door opened to a reveal a crouched, grey-haired, elderly man holding an oil lamp.

'Good evening. I believe this is the establishment of Dr Stapleford,' asked Ravenscroft giving a brief smile.

'Most likely it is, but Dr Stapleford is presently engaged,' replied the man, beginning to close the door once more.

'We are the police. It is most important that we have words with your master tonight,' said Ravenscroft quickly.

'That is not possible, sir. It is very late. My master is not available. You will have to make an appointment in the morning.'

'I insist that I see your master now on a most urgent matter. It is a question of life and death, and we must have an answer tonight,' urged Ravenscroft.

'This is most irregular.'

'But of the absolute importance, I can assure you.'

The manservant opened the door further and grudgingly beckoned the policemen to enter.

Ravenscroft and Crabb found themselves standing in a large hallway where faded photographs and portraits hung on the walls, and an almost threadbare carpet sought to cover the uneven stone floor. The manservant placed the lamp on a side table, before turning round and closing the long bolts on the door behind them.

'Thank you,' said Ravenscroft, as Crabb gave an uneasy glance at the bolted door.

'Follow me,' muttered the manservant, holding up the lamp and shuffling his way down a long corridor. 'You'll have to wait in there,' he instructed, opening the door to one of the rooms.

'I will see if Dr Stapleford will see you.'

'Thank you.'

The manservant closed the door behind him leaving the two policemen standing before a large table, upon which stood two lighted candelabra which illuminated the contents of the room.

'Good heavens!' exclaimed Crabb. 'What is inside all these glass jars?'

'Medical specimens, Tom, if I am not mistaken,' said Ravenscroft casting his eyes around the many shelves of bottles that lined the sides of the room.

'It's a shrivelled hand,' said Crabb, peering into one of the bottles.

'It does not seem as though its owner was in a healthy condition before he gave it up.'

'And this foot is all deformed. It's got six toes!' said a horrified Crabb. 'What are all these monstrous things doing here?'

'Medical research, I assume. Our doctor must have collected these specimens over a number of years,' said Ravenscroft, crossing over to the table to where a number of larger jars were to be found. 'This looks like a pair of lungs. In quite a bad way, I would say he or she was.'

'This is someone's heart,' said Crabb.

'This is what we all have inside us, Tom, although I would hope that we are in a better condition than some of these poor fellows,' said Ravenscroft peering at the specimens through the lenses of his spectacles.

'Well, I call it unnatural,' replied Crabb, lifting up one of the jars and studying its contents with some revulsion.

'I would be careful with that specimen if I were you, Constable; it is quite irreplaceable,' said a voice suddenly from behind them. Ravenscroft had been so absorbed that he had not noticed the grey-haired man who had just entered the room.

A startled Crabb hastily replaced the jar on the shelf.

'Doctor Stapleford, I presume?' asked Ravenscroft, observing that the doctor, a late middle-aged man in years, was dressed in a smoking jacket and grey trousers. He had a large scar running down the left-hand side of his face and his hair was of an untidy appearance.

'Your constable does not approve of my collection?' remarked Stapleford, ignoring Ravenscroft's question as he examined one of his specimens. 'But I sense you may be more tolerant of my work, Inspector. Do you know what this is?'

'A liver?'

'Exactly: it once belonged to a fifteen-year-old boy who lived in the slums of Shoreditch in London. It is quite decayed as you can see. The result of an over-dependence on gin, I would conclude. Sad, would you not agree? It seems such a waste of a life, and at such a young age as well. And that item over there — that is a foetus taken from a dead woman.'

'Doctor Stapleford, much as I agree that your specimens are no doubt of a fascinating nature—' began Ravenscroft.

'Oh, my dear sir, they are not just fascinating,' interrupted Stapleford. 'They are essential if medical science is to progress. Many people will no doubt be repulsed by my collection here, but if we are to cure the ills of the world, and advance in our medical understanding of such conditions, then it is essential that such research should be undertaken by men such as I who are at the forefront of medical advancement. You would not disagree with that premise, Inspector? Over here we have—'

'I am investigating the death of the young gentleman who was found by the river, here in Upton, two days ago,' interrupted Ravenscroft, taking a dislike to the condescending manner of the medical practitioner. 'I understand that you examined the deceased and issued the death certificate.'

'And your name is, sir?' enquired Stapleford.

'Detective Inspector Ravenscroft, and this is my associate, Constable Crabb,' replied the detective sensing that Stapleford was annoyed that his eloquent flow of words had been interrupted.

'Well, Ravenscroft, what do you want to know?' said Stapleford turning away. 'I am a busy man, and the hour is late, so I would be obliged if you would come straight to the point.'

'Can you confirm the cause of death for us?' asked Ravenscroft, determined not to be put off by the other's brisk manner.

'The man had clearly died as the result of a fall from his horse. There was extensive bruising at the back and to the rear of the head. But why do you want to know all this?'

'You have not heard what happened earlier this morning?'

'No. I have been here all day.'

'Well, sir, the unfortunate man was thought to be a Mr Simon Cleaves of Mathon Manor, but when he was buried it turned out that he was someone else,' said Crabb.

'What nonsense is this that your constable utters? The man speaks in riddles.'

'It is true, sir. When the dead man was found, everyone was under the impression that he was Mr Simon Cleaves. However, when the burial service took place earlier today, it was revealed that was not in fact his real name.'

'I don't see what all this has to do with me. I have never heard of this Cleaves person. It is of no consequence to me anyway as to what he was called. I just examined him and pronounced him dead. That is all I can say.'

'You have never had any previous contact with Mr Cleaves, or any member of his family?' asked Ravenscroft.

'What have I just said? Now, I have answered all your questions. I would be obliged if you would leave me to my research,' answered Stapleford, irritably, and striding over to the door.

'May I ask how you acquired these specimens sir?' asked Ravenscroft.

'Quite legally I can assure you, Inspector. I was engaged as a surgeon at Bart's Hospital in London for a number of years, until my move here to Upton some three years ago. Now, sir, if you would kindly leave. Parsons, will you show the inspector and the constable out.

'Well, our Dr Stapleford was an unpleasant fellow and no mistake,' said Ravenscroft as the trap headed back along the lane.

'What kind of man finds pleasure in bottling up parts of dead people?' asked Crabb.

'It could be as he said that he is just undertaking important medical research. I think he was lying, however, when he said that he had not had any contact with the Cleaves family. I would certainly like to know a lot more about the mysterious doctor. I think I will send a telegram to Bart's Hospital tomorrow morning and see what they can tell us about his activities there.'

'I am sure he has been up to no good.'

'I would also like to know how he acquired that rather ugly scar on his face. It was clearly an old wound. This certainly promises to be an interesting case. If the dead man was not Simon Cleaves, then who is he? And what was he doing with Simon Cleaves's watch and wallet on his person, to say nothing of the horse?' said Ravenscroft, deep in thought.

'The dead man could have killed Cleaves, taken his valuables and ridden off on his horse to Upton, where he met with an accident and was killed when he fell?' suggested Crabb.

'That could indeed be so, but if that was the case why has Mr Cleaves's body not been found yet?'

'Could be at the bottom of the River Severn.'

'Yes, but there is another possibility that Cleaves himself killed this man and then planted those personal items on the corpse before effecting his own disappearance.'

'Why would he do that?'

'To escape, or hide from someone, or something. Either way we will need to visit Mathon Manor tomorrow and interview the family. Who knows — by then perhaps Simon Cleaves himself may have returned.'

'Or his body will have been found?'

'In the meantime, Tom, we need to find out who the dead man is, and what he was doing here in Upton when he was killed, however it is far too late for us to do anymore now, so I think all that can all wait until tomorrow. Let us make our way back to home to Ledbury. Urge the horse forward if you will, Tom.'

CHAPTER TWO

MATHON MANOR

'Hoskings! Hoskings!' called out Ravenscroft loudly, as he strode into the front office of the Upton Police Station the following morning. 'Confound the man, where is he?'

'Probably still in bed, sir,' suggested Crabb sarcastically.

The door of the inner room opened suddenly and the flustered policeman entered the room.

'Ah, there you are, Hoskings. Has there been any news concerning our unknown corpse?' asked Ravenscroft.

'None at all, sir.'

'Right, Hoskings, I believe there should be some photographs for me?'

'Photographs, sir?'

'Yes, man. You did instruct the photographer to visit Shortcross and Maudlin to take some pictures of the dead man?'

'Yes, sir.'

'Well, where are the photographs then?' said Ravenscroft, annoyed by the lacklustre attitude of the policeman.

'Oh, yes, sir, the photographs, sir. Yes, they are here somewhere,' replied the constable frantically searching through a pile of papers beneath the counter.

'Yes, come on, Hoskings. We haven't got all day.'

'Ah, here they are, sir. Gentleman delivered them about thirty minutes ago,' said Hoskins, passing over a large envelope to his superior.

'Not a bad likeness I suppose considering the darkness in that room,' said Ravenscroft studying the photographs. 'Right now, Hoskings, I want you to put up one of these photographs outside the station, together with a notice asking if anyone knows who this man is.'

'Yes, sir.'

'Then I want you to visit all the inns, boarding-houses and drinking establishments in the town and show this photograph to as many people as possible. The man may have recently arrived in the town, but he could have been staying somewhere before his death.'

'Yes, sir.'

'Before that, however, I want you to send another one of the photographs to police headquarters in Worcester, together with this note I have written about the case. You understand, Hoskings?'

'Yes, sir.'

'Then, if you have any time left, and no one has been able to identify the man, then you are to visit all the shops and businesses in the town and see if anyone there can lay claim to having seen him. In the meantime, Constable Crabb and myself will travel over to Malvern where we will issue a description of the man to the local newspaper, before going on to Mathon to interview Lady Cleaves and her niece. We hope to return later this afternoon.'

'Yes, sir; right, sir.'

'And, Hoskings, when are you going to do those buttons up on your tunic in the correct order?' sighed Ravenscroft.

'Oh, sorry, sir, I will do it right away, sir.'

'Come, Tom, we have a busy day ahead of us, but before then we will visit the telegraph office and dispatch this message off to Bart's Hospital. If Dr Stapleford is hiding anything in his past then I mean to get to the bottom of it.'

* * *

After travelling the four or so miles to Great Malvern and visiting the local newspaper offices, Crabb and Ravenscroft found themselves taking the cutting between the hills, before their trap took them downwards and along narrow country lanes towards the village of Mathon.

'I believe this must be where the Cleaves family lives,' said Ravenscroft presently, as the trap pulled up outside a lodge gate on the right-hand side of road.

Crabb turned the horse and they soon found themselves travelling along a long driveway, with neatly landscaped lawns on either side of an avenue of larch trees, coming to a halt outside a fine Georgian country house.

As Ravenscroft alighted from the trap the main door of the residence opened and a tall, thin, grey-haired manservant came forward to meet the two policemen.

'Good day to you, sir, and how may I be of assistance to you?' enquired the servant.

'My name is Detective Inspector Ravenscroft and this is Constable Crabb. We have come to make inquiries of your mistress concerning yesterday's strange events,' said Ravenscroft.

'A most distressing business, sir, if I may say so,' replied the man shaking his head.

'You were there, Mr . . . er . . .'

'Mansfield, sir; I am the butler at Mathon Manor. Yes, I was present at the service. I must say that I was somewhat relieved when it was discovered that the dead man was not the master. Nevertheless, it was a most unsettling occasion for us all. I don't suppose you have any news of the master?'

'I am afraid not, Mr Mansfield. I am hoping that someone here may be able to cast some light on this matter.'

'Perhaps you would care to enter, sir, and I will see if someone is available to see you.' said the butler, indicating that Ravenscroft and Crabb should follow him up the flight of steps to the front entrance of the house.

As the two policemen entered the large hall, Ravenscroft looked up at the fine paintings and portraits hanging on the walls and onward up the long sweeping staircase.

'If you would wait in here, gentlemen, I am sure that Mr Webster will be with you presently,' said Mansfield, opening the door to one of the rooms.

'This is certainly a fine place,' said Crabb, looking around the drawing room with its booked-lined cases and mahogany furniture, after the butler had closed the door behind them.

'Yes. What a magnificent view. The family clearly have money. There are enough leather-bound volumes here to keep one occupied for at least a hundred years,' added Ravenscroft.

'Mrs Crabb would quite like some of this porcelain,' said Crabb examining one of the ornately decorated cups.

'I know Mrs Ravenscroft certainly would.'

'Gentlemen, I am sorry to have kept you waiting.'

The speaker was a middle-aged, fair-haired man who had just entered the room. 'I understand that you are from the local police?'

'Yes. I am Detective Inspector Ravenscroft and this is Constable Crabb. We are investigating the strange events of yesterday, sir. May I enquire with whom I am speaking?' asked Ravenscroft, observing that the new arrival was immaculately dressed, with a gold fob watch dangling from his brightly red waistcoat pocket, and what also appeared to be a gold and diamond tie pin in his cravat.

'Gervase Webster. I am Miss Cleaves's cousin,' replied the man, in a dry formal tone of voice.

'You were present at the burial service yesterday?' enquired Ravenscroft.

'No, I am afraid I was unable to attend. I received a telegram from my cousin, sent the previous evening, informing me of the sad event, but I did not arrive until late yesterday evening.'

'Oh, why was that, sir?'

'I am a barrister in the Inner Temple in London. I had an urgent court appearance at the Old Bailey, which I was unable to conclude to a satisfactory outcome until late in the afternoon.'

'I see, sir.'

'As soon as I arrived here I was of course informed of the morning's dramatic turn of events, by my cousin and my aunt, Lady Cleaves. I had naturally assumed that it was Simon who had died, so it came as something of a surprise to learn that was not the case.'

'Do you have any idea where your cousin, Mr Cleaves, might be now, sir?'

'I am afraid I have no idea, Inspector,' replied the barrister, allowing himself a brief smile.

'I wonder if it would be possible to speak to both Lady Cleaves and Miss Cleaves today?' asked Ravenscroft hopefully.

'I am afraid that might not be possible. Both my aunt and my cousin are very much distressed by all this business, as I am sure you will appreciate, Inspector,' replied Webster, adopting what Ravenscroft considered to be the same defensive manner which he had witnessed in the past in his dealings with some members of the legal fraternity in the law courts of London.

'I understand your concern, sir, but it is most essential to our enquiries that I have words with the two ladies today.'

'And I have told you, Inspector, that they do not wish to be disturbed. Now, I am sure that if you were to return tomorrow they may be able to assist you then,' replied Webster with an air of finality in his voice as he crossed over towards the door.

'I wonder if you would be kind enough to look at this photograph, sir,' said Ravenscroft, determined not to be intimidated.

Webster returned and took the photograph which Ravenscroft held before him.

'I take it that this is the dead man?' asked Webster.

'It is. Have you ever seen him before?'

'No,' replied the lawyer, casually handing the photograph back.

'Do you possibly have a photograph of Mr Simon Cleaves?'

'Why?'

'As your cousin is missing, sir, it may be of assistance to us in our inquiries.'

'I do not believe that my cousin is missing. I am sure there is a perfect explanation for his absence. He may well soon return.'

'Nevertheless, it would be of great benefit to us,' insisted Ravenscroft.

Webster stared at Ravenscroft briefly before looking around the room. 'There is this photograph of my cousin,' he said presently, holding up a silver frame. 'It was probably taken sometime within the past three to five years.'

'Do you consider it a good likeness, sir?'

'As good as any photograph I suppose. I will remove it from the frame.'

'Thank you, your assistance is much appreciated,' said Ravenscroft, placatingly as he accepted the photograph.

'—and as I was saying, my dear, a visit to London once this business is over will be of great—'

Ravenscroft turned to see that the door had opened suddenly, and that the speaker was an elderly lady who had just entered the room.

'Who are these gentlemen Gervase?' enquired a younger woman, of pale complexion, who accompanied the older lady.

'These gentlemen are the police making enquiries concerning the burial service yesterday,' said the lawyer.

'I am Detective Inspector Ravenscroft and my colleague is Constable Crabb,' interrupted Ravenscroft.

'I told the gentlemen that you were both indisposed. I believe they were just about to leave,' said Webster somewhat dismissively.

'I would be obliged, Lady Cleaves, Miss Cleaves, for a few minutes of your valuable time,' continued Ravenscroft. 'I appreciate the distress that yesterday's events may have caused you both, but it is imperative that we learn as much as we can about the situation. An unknown man was nearly buried in mistake for your nephew Lady Cleaves. We have to know why.'

'I suppose it will do no harm,' sighed Lady Cleaves, seating herself on one of the chairs.

'Aunt, I am sure they can return tomorrow,' offered Anne Cleaves in some concern.

'Time is of the essence, ladies. We cannot bury this poor unfortunate man until we have established his identity,' said Ravenscroft, determined not to be thwarted.

'I see no reason to object, Anne,' replied Lady Cleaves. 'After all, your brother has been missing for over two weeks now.'

'Thank you, Lady Cleaves.'

As Ravenscroft seated himself on one of the chairs, he studied the two ladies before him; the older one, tall, erect and unsmiling, looked at him with disdain; the younger one was pale and drawn and nervous in manner.

'I am sure that Simon will return quite soon,' said Anne.

'When did you last see your brother, Miss Cleaves?' asked Ravenscroft, addressing the younger woman.

'As my aunt has just said, Inspector, Simon left just over two weeks ago.'

'Did he say where he was going, or how long he would be away for?' continued Ravenscroft.

'No. He did not say.'

'Is it usual for your brother to be absent for so long?'

'He has been known to be away on business for some weeks at a time.'

'And you do not know what the nature of this business was?'

'No. My brother did not confide in me regarding his business activities.'

'Look, Inspector, I really think all this is enough. My cousin has given you her answers,' interrupted Webster clearly annoyed that Ravenscroft had not left sooner.

'According to Mr Midwinter, I understand, Lady Cleaves, that you heard noises from within the coffin,' pressed Ravenscroft.

'Yes. I was quite sure, at the time, that I had heard a noise that seemed to come from inside the coffin, but evidently I was mistaken,' answered the lady looking somewhat embarrassed.

'And you, Miss Cleaves?'

'I heard nothing, Inspector.'

'It must have been something else that I had heard in the graveyard. It was very windy there, and it had just begun to rain,' added Lady Cleaves.

'I wonder if you would both be kind enough to look at this photograph for me,' said Ravenscroft, passing over the item for Anne Cleaves to study.

'Really, Ravenscroft, this is too much. My cousin and aunt have suffered a terrible experience, which you now seek to rekindle by this action,' protested the lawyer.

'I am sorry, sir, but we are making great efforts to try and establish the identity of this man and, as such, we need to ask as many people as we—' began Ravenscroft.

'But my aunt and cousin have already seen this man yesterday in that coffin,' protested Webster.

'It is all right, Gervase,' said Lady Cleaves staring at the photograph through a magnifying glass which she had picked up from the table beside her. 'I have never seen this man before.'

'And you, Miss Cleaves?'

'No,' replied Anne handing the photograph back to Ravenscroft.

'Can you think of any reason why this man would have had your brother's watch and wallet on his person?'

'No.'

'Your brother had not mentioned that they were missing, before his departure?' asked Ravenscroft, observing that the young lady was entwining her fingers nervously in her lap.

'No,' replied Anne.

'The house has not been entered by any strange people of late?'

'Not as I am aware.'

'I think that is enough,' interceded Webster again.

'Thank you all for your assistance. We will take our leave. As Mr Cleaves is apparently missing I will inform my colleagues of his disappearance, and we will, of course, keep you fully informed of any developments in our inquiries,' said Ravenscroft, getting up to leave.

'As I have said, Inspector, I am sure that there is a logical reason for my brother's absence. I am sure he will return quite soon,' said Anne Cleaves.

'I trust you are right, Miss Cleaves. Should your brother return in the meantime I would be obliged if you would send word to the police station in Upton. We will need to question him regarding his missing items.'

'Of course, Inspector,' replied Anne giving a slight smile.

'Good day, Lady Cleaves. Miss Cleaves. Mr Webster.'

* * *

'Miss Cleaves didn't seem particularly concerned by her brother's absence,' remarked Crabb, as the trap made its way back along the drive.

'You are right, Tom. A man goes missing for two weeks, and no one knows where he has gone to, or when he intends to return. I do not believe her lack of concern. The family seemed to accept that Simon Cleaves had been found dead in Upton on Saturday, and yet today they are inclined to persist with this tale that he is about to return quite soon. Something is not quite right,' replied Ravenscroft casting a backward glance as the house disappeared from view.

'Strange that old Lady Cleaves thought that she had heard sounds from within that coffin, and yet, according to Mr Midwinter, no one else heard them.'

'Yes, it does strike one as being rather odd. She was evidently mistaken as the man was found to be quite dead when they opened the coffin. It may be as she stated, that the noise could have come from somewhere else in the churchyard. The weather was bad, and the mind can play strange tricks in those circumstances. Still, it is fortunate that she did insist on opening the coffin; otherwise the unknown man would have been buried in her nephew's place, and we would not then have had a case to investigate.'

'I can't say I took to that gent Webster.'

'I think he was just being over protective in respect to his cousin and aunt. That is understandable. He certainly has a formal, slightly disparaging manner, but that no doubt comes from his many years at the Bar.'

'What will we do now, sir?' asked Crabb.

'Return to Upton and see if Hoskings has found anyone who has been able to identify the dead man. Until we have a name to fit the face, I cannot see how we can proceed further with this case.'

CHAPTER THREE

GLENFOREST

The following morning found Ravenscroft and Lucy taking the long winding road from Ledbury, through the nearby villages of Bosbury and Bishop's Frome, towards the Herefordshire market town of Bromyard.

Ravenscroft had returned to Upton the previous afternoon after his visit to Mathon Manor, but the news had not been good. Despite all of Hoskings's enquiries in the town, no one had admitted to having either known, or seen, the dead man. Furthermore, neither his letter to the police station in Worcester requesting any known information or sightings of the man, nor his telegram sent to Bart's Hospital in London regarding Stapleford, had yet to yield a result.

'I can tell that you are very preoccupied with this case,' remarked Lucy, after a long period of silence.

'Oh, I am sorry. My thoughts were elsewhere,' answered her husband.

'We can always go another day. I can send our apologies to Mr Smeaton.'

'No, that will not be necessary, for to tell you the truth until we have established this man's identity we cannot do anymore. I have sent both Tom and Hoskings to widen the search in some of the nearby villages. The man must have come from somewhere. What on earth was he doing in Upton that day? I still don't know whether he died as the result of an accident, or whether we should consider that someone deliberately killed him.'

'It was strange that he had Simon Cleaves's possessions on his person.'

'Yes, and that is the mystery about this whole thing.'

'And there has been no word about this Mr Cleaves?'

'No, I'm afraid not. It would certainly be very convenient if he were to turn up now.'

'Oh look, Samuel, that must be Bromyard over there,' said Lucy pointing in the distance towards some buildings on top of a hill.

Ravenscroft halted the horse by a group of men who were standing by the side of the road, and made enquiries regarding Glenforest School.

'That be a place for toff's sons,' remarked one of the men, laughing to his companions.

'Ye needs a bag of money to goes there, and no mistake,' joked the second man.

'If ye goes up the road towards the common for about a mile, ye will find it on the right-hand side,' added the third.

'Thank you, my man,' said Ravenscroft, urging the horse up the steep hill.

A few minutes later Ravenscroft and Lucy found themselves standing outside a large, unassuming, brick-built building situated a few feet from the side of the road.

'A rather forbidding exterior,' remarked Ravenscroft. 'But they say you should never judge a bottle until you have sampled its contents.'

'I think it is in quite a nice position, with the Downs all around,' said Lucy optimistically.

Ravenscroft rang the doorbell and presently was rewarded by the arrival of a small, dark-haired man who squinted at them through rounded pebbled spectacles.

'We have called to see Mr Horace Smeaton,' said Ravenscroft, smiling, as he removed his hat.

'I am he, sir. I am the Principal of Glenforest,' replied the man.

'I am Mr Ravenscroft and this is my wife Mrs Ravenscroft.'

'Yes, I suppose you are,' said the man looking somewhat flustered.

'We have an appointment to see the school,' persisted Ravenscroft, aware that the man's upper teeth appeared to be too large for his mouth.

'This morning? Oh dear me.'

'I sent you a letter,' said Lucy.

'Of course you did. Then you had better come in. Mr and Mrs Ravenswood, you say?' said Smeaton throwing open the door.

'Ravenscroft,' corrected the detective.

'Of course. Absolutely. If you would both care to follow me, we will see what can be done.'

They followed Smeaton through a dingy hallway, and into a book-lined study that was situated at the back of the building.

'Do please take a seat, Mrs . . . er . . .' began Smeaton, removing a pile of papers from a chair before a large desk.

'Thank you,' said Lucy accepting the seat.

'If you would care to sit over there, my dear sir,' said the headmaster indicating another chair, before seating himself behind the desk. 'Now then, where are we?' asked Smeaton, looking through a large pile of papers on his desk. 'Yes, here we are. Your son; young Robert, I believe?'

'Richard,' corrected Lucy.

'Yes, of course. Richard. I believe your letter stated that your son was eight years of age?' continued Smeaton moving his spectacles towards the top of his head before peering at a page before him.

'Our son is six,' replied Lucy, somewhat disconcerted by the headmaster's confusion.

'Absolutely! Yes, of course. Well, what can I tell you about Glenforest?'

'Well—' began Ravenscroft.

'We have approximately sixty boys here. Our youngest is five years of age; our oldest is thirteen. We run a very tight, strict school. Our children receive a thorough grounding in English, Mathematics, Latin and Greek, and we pride ourselves on our English History syllabus. That is my speciality. Games are another of our subjects. Cross-country running four times a week, early morning exercises on the Downs, walks into the town on a Sunday to attend church. We are very fortunate in our situation here, as you will no doubt have observed. We believe that a healthy body produces a healthy mind. Many of our pupils go on to public schools such as Malvern College. You know Malvern College, Mr Ravens — er. . .? We even had one boy last year who went on to win a scholarship to Winchester. Not a mean feat, I can assure you.'

'I wonder whether it would be possible to view the school?' asked Ravenscroft, deciding that it was time to interrupt the academic's flow of words.

'View the school?' peered Smeaton lowering his spectacles down onto his nose and staring hard at him. 'View the school? That would be most irregular, my dear sir, I can assure you; most irregular.'

'Why?' asked Lucy.

'It would be detrimental to the children's concentration during their lessons, my dear lady. No, it will certainly not do at all.'

'Then I think we may have been wasting your time, Mr Smeaton,' replied Ravenscroft quickly rising from his seat.

'Not so hasty, my dear sir. I can appreciate your curiosity. If you insist, I think we might perhaps visit one of the classrooms, if only for a little while,' said Smeaton standing up from behind his desk. 'If you would both care to follow me.'

The head teacher lead the way up a long flight of winding stairs, pausing eventually outside one of the rooms on the landing.

'This is Mr Choke's class,' pronounced Smeaton before opening the door.

As Ravenscroft and Lucy entered the airless classroom they were met by the sound of desk seats being raised.

'Our profound apologies for the interruption, Mr Choke, but Mr and Mrs Ravenswood have expressed an interest in seeing one our classes,' said Smeaton casting his eyes at the rows of boys.

'Good afternoon,' said Ravenscroft addressing the young teacher.

'Good afternoon, sir.'

'And what are our charges learning today, Mr Choke?' asked Smeaton.

'The kings and queens of England, Headmaster,' replied the teacher.

'Capital! That is a subject after my own heart. Here, you boy, Harrison,' said Smeaton, pointing to a particularly tall boy in the back row. 'Tell me who succeeded Charles II?'

'It's Rackstraw, sir,' corrected the boy.

'Yes, yes, that is all very well, Rackstraw, but answer the question, boy, just answer the question,' demanded an irritated Smeaton.

'Er . . . er . . .' stuttered the boy seeking to avoid the headmaster's stare by casting his eyes up at the ceiling.

'Well, come on, Rackstraw,' sighed Smeaton. 'We are all waiting for your reply.'

'Charles the Third, sir,' replied the boy, much to the amusement of his classmates.

'Silence!' bellowed Smeaton. 'I think you had better see me later, Rackstraw, for some extra tuition. Silly boy! It would seem, Mr Choke, that your charges have learned very little this morning.'

'I am sorry, Headmaster,' said Choke, sheepishly.

'I think it would be better if we were to leave Mr Choke to continue with his lesson,' said Smeaton, ushering Ravenscroft and Lucy from the room, before either of them could say their farewells to the teacher.

'I can only apologize for that boy's ignorance. Not a particularly bright specimen I'm afraid, but he has not been with us for very long, and we have high hopes for him in the future, of course,' said Smeaton, leading the way hastily down the main staircase. Ravenscroft and Lucy followed on in silence, not knowing quite what to say to one another.

'Now then,' said Smeaton, when they had reached the outside of his study once more. 'When were you considering sending your little . . . er . . . Robert here, er . . . Mr . . .? Yes, quite. Our numbers are quite limited at the moment. We have a long waiting list, but I am sure if you wanted your young son to commence here as soon as possible, then I dare say that we could accommodate him. '

'Good Lord!' exclaimed Ravenscroft, looking at one of the school photographs on the wall.

'I am sorry?' said a startled Smeaton.

'Tell me, Mr Smeaton, when was this photograph taken?' asked Ravenscroft.

'About three months ago, my dear sir, but I don't understand your interest. It is just the annual photograph we have taken of all the masters and boys.'

'And who is this man on the end of the back row?' asked Ravenscroft, pointing to one of the figures.

'Oh that was Mr Smith, one of our teachers. He had not been with us for very long when the photograph was taken,' answered Smeaton, after pressing his face close up to the frame.

'I take it Mr Smith is no longer with you?'

'Er . . . yes, that is so, but how did you know that?'

'How long did Mr Smith teach here?' asked Ravenscroft ignoring the headmaster's last question.

'He was with us for about six months, I believe.'

'And when did he leave the school?'

'He left somewhat unexpectedly; it was last Friday evening,' replied a puzzled Smeaton.

'Mr Smith did not say where he was going?'

'Er, no, as I have just said, he left quite suddenly. He was not present at breakfast on Saturday morning, and when Mr

Choke went up to his room he found that he was not there. He must have left during the night. I have to tell you that we were all most put out by such unsatisfactory conduct. Leaving without giving notice is most unacceptable.'

The headmaster's words were interrupted by a loud bell ringing somewhere on the landing above their heads, followed by a violent banging of doors and the noise of children shouting.

'I am afraid I have some very bad news for you, Mr Smeaton—' began the detective, as a group of noisy boys ran down the stairs and began pushing past them.

'Boys, boys, if you please!' shouted Smeaton, above the noise. 'If you will, boys, do not forget who you are. Decorum at all times!'

'I have to inform you, Mr Smeaton, that Mr Smith has been found dead,' announced Ravenscroft, noticing that the young teacher, Choke, was also making his way down the stairs.

'Dead! You say dead? Dear me. Mr Choke, I have just been informed of some terrible news. Poor Smith is dead,' said Smeaton.

'Smith, dead?' repeated Choke, as Ravenscroft noticed the colour suddenly draining away from the schoolmaster's face.

'Yes, I am afraid I have to tell you that Mr Smith was found dead on Saturday afternoon, at Upton-upon-Severn. We believe that he died as the result of a fall from a horse.'

'No, that cannot be so,' said Smeaton. 'You must have the wrong man. Smith did not ride horses, as far as we know.'

'Perhaps if you would both care to look at this photograph,' said Ravenscroft reaching into his pocket. 'And tell me whether this gentleman was your teacher Mr Smith.'

'Oh my dear!' exclaimed Smeaton.

'Yes, that is poor John, but I do not understand,' said Choke.

'This is perfectly dreadful news, but what is your interest in this matter, my dear sir?' asked Smeaton.

'I am Detective Inspector Ravenscroft, and at present I am investigating the death of this man, your Mr Smith. Until now we have been unable to put a name to him, as he had no papers of identification upon him.'

'I see,' said Smeaton.

'So, if you could tell me all you know about this John Smith I would be most obliged.'

'Well, Inspector, as I have just said, Mr Smith came to us about six months ago. He replied to an advertisement I had placed in *The Times*, and after a short interview I decided to offer him the situation; for a trial period you understand.'

'Did Mr Smith provide any references?'

'No, but he told me he had previously trained for the legal profession, in London I believe, and as he seemed such a presentable young man, I thought he might be suitable here at Glenforest,' answered Smeaton.

'When Mr Smith's body was discovered there was no means of identification upon him, as I have just said, but we did find that he had in his possession a watch and a wallet containing papers which had belonged to a Mr Simon Cleaves. I wonder whether this gentleman's name means anything to either of you?' asked Ravenscroft.

'No,' said Choke.

'The name Simon Cleaves means nothing to me, but Miss Cleaves has visited the school quite recently,' offered Smeaton.

'A Miss Anne Cleaves of Mathon Manor?' said Ravenscroft surprised.

'Well, yes,' answered the headmaster.

'May I enquire what Miss Cleaves's interest was in the school?'

'The Cleaves family has often awarded scholarships for young boys of their parish. She visited the school to see what facilities we could offer such children. You may recall the lady, Marcus?'

'Oh yes, Headmaster, I remember her visit very well,' said Choke.

'That is very interesting. Do you recall whether Miss Cleaves encountered Mr Smith during her visit to the school?' continued Ravenscroft, relieved that he had at last established the identity of the unknown man.

'I do not believe so. Choke?'

'No, Headmaster. I think the young lady spoke only with you, and myself.'

'I would be obliged if I could view the room where Mr Smith slept? Perhaps Mr Choke could assist me?' asked Ravenscroft.

'Yes, of course,' replied Choke.

'Thank you, Mr Smeaton, you have been most helpful. Would you like to lead the way, Mr Choke?'

'I will wait for you in the trap, Samuel,' said Lucy.

'Allow me to escort you, my dear Mrs Ravenswood,' offered Smeaton smiling through his large teeth.

Lucy gave her husband an uneasy smile as she accepted the headmaster's arm.

Ravenscroft followed Choke up the main staircase of the school.

'I'm afraid it is rather a climb, Inspector. Both John's room and my quarters are on the very top floor of the building,' said the schoolmaster.

After gaining the main landing, outside the schoolroom which Ravenscroft had entered a few minutes previously, the two men climbed another, much narrower staircase, which lead onto another landing.

'These are the dormitories where the boys sleep,' said Choke. I am afraid there is still another flight.'

Yet more steps took Ravenscroft and the teacher onto a smaller landing, which Ravenscroft guessed was built into the eaves of the building, where two doors now faced them.

'That is my room over there. Poor John slept in this room,' said Choke opening the door.

Ravenscroft found himself standing in a small, dismal, unappealing room where the only light came from a darkened, dirty window that had been inserted at some stage into the sloping roof.

'I'm afraid you won't find anything here, Inspector. I think John must have taken all his personal things with him when he left us,' said Choke, as Ravenscroft began to open the drawers of the bedside cabinet.

'Can you tell me anything else about Mr Smith? He must have confided in you,' asked Ravenscroft, next turning his attention to the wardrobe in the corner of the room.

'John, Mr Smith, was a man who spoke very little about his affairs. He kept himself very much to himself. I believe he once mentioned that he had trained for the Bar in London, but that he had failed to complete his studies, and that he had consequently been unable to obtain any work. Then one day he saw Mr Smeaton's advertisement and applied for the position. That is all I can tell you.'

'Did he ever receive any visitors?'

'No, I believe not — Mr Smeaton does not encourage members of staff to have visits from either friends or relations.'

'Did he ever receive letters?' continued Ravenscroft, kneeling down and looking under the bed.

'I don't recall him ever having received any communications. He must have been quite alone in the world. It is rather sad, I suppose.'

'I think you are right, Mr Choke, when you say that Mr Smith took all his possessions with him when he left,' said Ravenscroft, concluding his fruitless search. 'When was the last time you saw him?'

'It was late on Friday evening. We were both sitting in the library, when John said he was going to retire for the evening.'

'What time was that?'

'Around nine o'clock, I think.'

'And what time did you retire?'

'About ten-fifteen.'

'And when you came up here did you hear any noise from Mr Smith's room?'

'No.'

'Did you hear any noises during the night?'

'No, but then I am a heavy sleeper.'

'Can you tell me what happened on Saturday morning?'

'Well, I rose at six-thirty, washed, dressed, then, as it was my turn, I went to the dormitories and roused the boys, after which I went down for breakfast. It was then about fifteen minutes past seven. There was no sign of Smith, so Mr Smeaton asked me to go and see if he was unwell. So I came up here, and when I knocked on the door and heard no reply, I came inside, and that was when I discovered that he had left.'

'So Mr Smith must have left the school sometime after nine on Friday evening, and before, say, half past six on Saturday morning?'

'I suppose that must be correct, Inspector.'

'And you are sure that you neither heard, nor saw anything suspicious during that time?'

'No. I am sorry, I cannot help you further, Inspector.'

'On the contrary, you have been most informative, Mr Choke. One final question: have you ever met Mr Simon Cleaves of Mathon Manor?'

'No. As Mr Smeaton has stated, I only met Miss Cleaves, when she visited the school.'

'Thank you, Mr Choke,' said Ravenscroft, beginning to take his leave.

'May I ask where John's body is now?' asked Choke.

'It is with the undertakers in Upton.'

'And what will happen to him?'

'Well, now that we have established his identity, and I have informed the coroner, I see no reason why he cannot be buried as soon as possible.'

'I should like to pay for John's funeral. I have little savings, but I would like also to pay for a stone. I think John must have been quite alone in this world. I would not like him to be buried in an unmarked grave. One day, someone may wish to claim him as their own,' said Choke, speaking quietly, and with feeling.

'That is most generous of you, Mr Choke, and most commendable,' replied Ravenscroft, touched by the young schoolmaster's sincerity.

'It is the least I can do.'

* * *

Later that afternoon as the two detectives made their way back to Mathon Manor, Ravenscroft considered the dramatic events of the morning. He had now established the identity of the dead man, and had accounted for his movements for the six months prior to his death, but this revelation had thrown up more problems than it had solved, for Smith — if indeed that was his real name — had been revealed as a somewhat lonely figure, about which little had been known, other than the fact that he had trained as a lawyer in London prior to his engagement at Glenforest. Then he had unexpectedly and suddenly disappeared, without informing anyone of his impending departure, leaving in the middle of the night, taking all his possessions with him, and then being found dead by the river, some ten or more miles away, on the following afternoon, with another man's personal items in his pockets.

He had learned that Anne Cleaves had recently visited the school. Both Smeaton and Choke had stated that Smith had not met their visitor, but then they could have been mistaken. Had Smith and Anne Cleaves met after all? Had they even met before, in London perhaps, and if so, what was their connection? In which case, Anne Cleaves would have been lying when she said that she had never seen the man before.

Had the schoolteacher Smith known Simon Cleaves? Had the two men arranged to meet, and had there then been an altercation of some sort, when Smith had killed Cleaves and taken possession of his personal effects, but if that was the case why had they not found Simon Cleaves's body? And why had the young landowner left his home in the first place, two weeks before, without telling anyone where he was going and when he would return?

He felt sure that Anne Cleaves could now provide him with the answers he sought. Furthermore he also hoped that he would be able to question Gervase Webster as the lawyer might be able to provide him with valuable information concerning the private affairs of the family.

'Good day to you, Mr Ravenscroft,' said the elderly butler, as Ravenscroft and Crabb walked up the steps to the main entrance of the building.

'Good afternoon to you, Mansfield,' replied Ravenscroft.

'May I enquire whether you have any news concerning the master?'

'I am afraid not, but all the authorities have been alerted. I wonder whether it would be possible to speak to Mr Webster.'

'I am afraid Mr Webster returned to London yesterday evening.'

'Oh that is a pity,' replied Ravenscroft. 'I wonder if I might then speak to Miss Cleaves?'

'If you and your constable would care to wait in the drawing room I will inform the mistress of your arrival.'

'Thank you, Mansfield.'

'Rather unfortunate,' remarked Crabb, while the two men waited.

'You are referring to Webster? Yes, I was rather hoping that he might provide us with some valuable information regarding his cousin's affairs.'

The door opened and Anne Cleaves entered.

'Good afternoon to you, Miss Cleaves,' said Ravenscroft turning the face the young woman.

'I am afraid my aunt cannot see you, as she is resting at present, and I should not like to disturb her. You have no doubt also heard that Mr Webster has returned to London,' said Anne speaking in a voice that was scarcely audible.

'Indeed, Miss Cleaves, but it is you that we have called to see,' said Ravenscroft, observing that the young woman looked pale and drawn.

'I hope that you do not bring us bad news concerning my brother?'

'No, Miss Cleaves, I am afraid I still have no information about Mr Cleaves.'

'Please take a seat, Inspector. Perhaps you would like some tea?' asked their hostess seating herself on the sofa.

'That will not be necessary, Miss Cleaves, but I thank you for your kind offer. I have to tell you that I find it difficult to accept that you are completely unaware of your brother's activities,' said Ravenscroft, deciding that it was better to come directly to the point, so that he could observe the young woman's reactions.

'I am sorry for that, but that is the case. As I have said before, my brother does not confide in me,' replied Anne, defensively.

'Do you know whether your brother has any gambling or sporting debts?'

'Not as far as I am aware.'

'When your brother has left home in the past, have you been aware of where he might have been going?'

'He sometimes visits friends in Bath, and often he goes on business to London.'

'Oh, and what kind of business would that be, Miss Cleaves?'

'I do not know. Perhaps you should ask my cousin, Mr Webster. He may be able to assist you in that concern.'

'And have you contacted these friends in Bath, to see if he is there?'

'I do not know all of my brother's friends and associates, but yes I have contacted all those that I know, but they have not seen him.'

'When did you visit Glenforest School near Bromyard?' asked Ravenscroft, changing the subject of their conversation, after realizing that his hostess seemed unprepared, or unwilling, to give him the answers he required relating to her brother's interests.

'I am sorry. I don't understand what that has to do with my brother,' replied Anne startled by the question.

'Mr Smeaton, the Principal, told me of your visit,' continued Ravenscroft, ignoring the question.

'I went there about a month ago. Our family has always tried to assist the children of the village, and one of the ways in which we can do that is to send one or two boys, who show promise, to a private school, so that they may benefit from a sound education and be given a good start in life.'

'Can't the village school do that, miss?' asked Crabb, looking up from his pocket book, where he had been making notes.

'We find that the children only receive a limited education at the village school. But what is all this to do with my brother?'

'We have identified the dead man as a certain John Smith, who was a teacher at Glenforest School,' announced Ravenscroft, aware that the lady was beginning to show signs of irritation.

'I see — and what is this to do with me?'

'On your visit to the school did you meet Mr Smith?'

'No. I only spoke to Mr Smeaton. We did go into one of the classrooms. I think the teacher there was a Mr Childs, or Church.'

'Choke,' corrected Ravenscroft.

'Yes, that was it, a Mr Choke. I remember that he was most kind and informative. But I saw none of the other teachers at the school.'

'Does the name John Smith mean anything to you?'

'John Smith would seem to be a common enough name, but I cannot recall meeting anyone of that name.'

'Not on one of your visits to London?' suggested Ravenscroft.

'I do not go up to London very often, although I have had cause to visit my cousin, Mr Webster, in his chambers, on one or two occasions.'

'And what was the purpose of those visits, Miss Cleaves.'

'Really, Inspector, I am finding all your questions rather tedious. I visited Gervase to discuss matters of a family nature.

That is all I am prepared to say. Now, if you will excuse me,' she said rising quickly from her seat.

'So you did not see this Mr Smith on one of your visits to London?'

'If I had seen the gentleman, or if I had recognized the photograph of the dead man, I would have said so,' replied Anne. 'I think I have now answered all your questions.'

'Could you describe to us the day on which your brother left the house?' persisted Ravenscroft.

'I don't quite understand your question, Inspector.'

'Well, did your brother say anything to you as he left?'

'Simon just said that he had been called away on urgent business, and that he could not say how long he would be,' replied Anne nervously.

'He did not say what the nature of this urgent business was?'

'No. He gave instructions to the servants to have his horse saddled and bought to the front of the house, and then I watched him leave as he rode down the drive. And that was the last time I saw him.'

'Did he take an overnight bag, or any other luggage with him?'

'Yes, I believe he may have taken a small brown bag with him.'

'Thank you, Miss Cleaves. You have been most helpful. I will keep you fully informed of developments.'

* * *

'She was lying to us, Tom,' said Ravenscroft, as the trap began its journey down the drive.

'She is certainly hiding something,' added Crabb.

'I think she knows where her brother is, but for some reason she is not prepared to tell us. I suppose if her brother has gone into hiding from someone, or something, that would explain her reason for wanting to keep his whereabouts a secret.'

'She was very uneasy when you mentioned Glenforest School.'

'Yes, so you saw her reaction as well? I think she knew that the dead man was Smith, and, furthermore, I am convinced that they must have met together somewhere — either at Glenforest, or in London, perhaps even in Webster's chambers — but again she seemed not inclined to tell us the truth. The trouble is, Tom, I cannot prove anything against her.'

'We could take her in for more questioning. She might confess eventually and tell us all that we want to know,' suggested Crabb.

'I don't want to do that just yet. I also have a feeling that if we were to take her into custody, Gervase Webster would seek to prosecute us without delay. He is very defensive of his cousin.'

'So what do we do now, sir?'

'Go home, Tom. Tomorrow I intend to travel to London. I want to question Webster about his cousin Simon Cleaves, and about the family's affairs. He might know where his cousin is. John Smith trained as a barrister in London so perhaps someone there might remember him, and we can learn more about the man's past. Also as Bart's have not replied to my letter concerning Dr Stapleford, I intend paying them a visit.'

'It sounds as though you will have a busy day ahead of you, sir. What would you like Hoskings and me to do in your absence?' asked Crabb.

'Hoskings can continue to make inquiries in Upton, but I would like you to pay a visit to Bromyard. Take a copy of the photograph of the dead man and question the people there. See if they can provide us with any information regarding Smith. Maybe he met someone in one of the inns. See also if he met a lady on his days off. Someone might even have seen him leave Glenforest late at night. I don't know. See if there is any gossip in the town about either Smith, Smeaton and the school.'

'Right sir.'

'I believe, *I hope*, that after tomorrow, we may have the answers to this mystery.'

CHAPTER FOUR

LONDON

'Here you are, guvnor,' said the cabman pulling up his horse. 'That will be three of good Queen Victoria's pennies, if you please.'

'Thank you, my good man,' smiled Ravenscroft, as he climbed out of the cab. 'Keep the change.'

'Bless you sir, and all that you looks after.'

Ravenscroft was now standing at the busy junction of Fleet Street and Chancery Lane, and paused for a brief moment to look around him at the familiar sounds and sights he had once known during his days as a policeman in Whitechapel. He crossed over the road, avoiding the clusters of animal droppings on the ground and the many horse-drawn vehicles moving frantically in all directions, and sought the narrow unobtrusive entrance that he knew would take him into the Temple.

As he walked on the cobbled pavement down the lane, he passed by the old wigmaker's shop with its low ceilings and its ancient bowed, glass-fronted windows, and eventually found himself in a quiet square where the four-storey buildings seem to stretch forever upwards towards the sky. On his left Ravenscroft observed the twelfth-century Templar Church, with its round Gothic nave, which he knew contained the bones of the old Crusader knights. He had visited this area on several occasions over the years, usually to consult prosecuting lawyers, before the criminals he had apprehended appeared in court, and it never ceased to amaze him how a journey of only a hundred or so steps took him away from all the noise and bustle of the metropolis to this peaceful and quietly dignified place.

As he did not have a precise address for Gervase Webster, he knew that his only course of action would be to consult the many lists of names attached to the outside of each building, in the hope that he would find the one he sought.

After ten minutes of this labour, Ravenscroft was on the point of giving up his search when he was suddenly aware of someone standing behind him.

'It's no good you know. It's like finding a needle in a haystack.'

Ravenscroft turned round and saw that the speaker was a tall, young, sandy-haired gentleman.

'I think you are correct, sir,' replied Ravenscroft.

'Up from the country, are we?' laughed the stranger.

'Indeed,' confirmed Ravenscroft.

'Never visit the country unless I have to. All that grass, and all those endless boring forests of green trees! You hardly ever see any people, only animals that seem intent on disturbing one. Dangerous place the country. Do you know that when people visit the countryside they never seem to come back? Death lurks in every hedgerow and hay loft.'

Ravenscroft smiled, and decided that there was something he quite liked about the pleasant humour of this young man.

'If I am not mistaken, I see a man who is in need of a good barrister.'

'Well, yes, actually I am.'

'I knew it! As soon as I saw you studying that list of names I said to myself, there is a gentleman who needs legal advice.

Allow me to present you with my calling card — Muncaster, at your immediate service, sir. Timothy Muncaster newly called to the Bar,' said the young man, handing over his card.

'Ravenscroft. Samuel Ravenscroft.'

'Now, my dear sir, how may I be of assistance to you? It is surely not a matrimonial problem? You look too happy for that. No? Perhaps you have been swindled out of funds by some villainous fellow? No, I think not. Mistaken identity? Wrongful arrest a possibility? Whatever the nature of your personal difficulty, my dear sir, you can be assured that Muncaster will defend you to the best of his ability.'

'Actually I wonder if you have ever seen this man before?' asked Ravenscroft, taking out the photograph of the dead Smith and handing it over to the young lawyer.

'He looks rather dead,' said Muncaster pulling a face.

'He is.'

'I see.'

'We believe his name to be John Smith.'

'I cannot say that either the name, or photograph are known to me, but I sense that you are not in need of a good barrister on your own account?'

'You are correct, Mr Muncaster. I am a detective inspector and I am investigating the death of this man who was found dead in Upton-upon-Severn in Worcestershire.'

'Well, sir, you are a long way from home.'

'I have come here today to speak with Mr Gervase Webster, who may be able to assist me in my investigation,' said Ravenscroft taking back the photograph.

'Gervase, you say! You should have said so earlier.'

'You know Mr Webster?'

'Indeed I do, sir. I work on the floor above him. Everyone in the Temple knows Gervase Webster. He gets all the best briefs around here. We poor beginners search, often in vain, for the poor scraps which he discards. Do you know that there are ten barristers chasing each brief that becomes available in the Temple?'

'I would be obliged if you would tell me where his chambers are,' said Ravenscroft.

'Say no more, my dear sir. It is fortunate that we have met. I will conduct you there myself.'

'That would be much appreciated.'

'Follow me, Inspector, and please retain my card. You never know when you might have need of my services,' smiled Muncaster as the two men began to walk across the courtyard.

'I will indeed.'

'Here is something that might interest you, Inspector,' said Muncaster stopping suddenly as they turned the corner into another square. 'You see that window up there, with the drawn blind? That was where Jack the Ripper lived.'

'Really — and how do you know that?'

'Well, shortly before those infamous murders took place, we all heard that a mysterious tenant had moved into that room. I say mysterious because no one ever saw him at the Bailey, or even at one of the other courts, and he certainly never seemed to have any visitors or clients call upon him,' said Muncaster recounting his story with enthusiasm.

'Then if no one ever saw him, how did they ever know that he was Jack the Ripper?' asked Ravenscroft, curious to know more.

'Ah, well, several of the clerks recall seeing a night candle burning in the window there on the evenings when all those women were killed. He must have used those rooms as his hiding place after the murders, escaping from Whitechapel after he had committed his dastardly deeds by going down to the river, and making his way unobserved along the waters, before coming up through the Temple Gardens. Quite a handy refuge for a murderer, wouldn't you say? Shortly after the last murder took place, and our mysterious friend had not been seen for some days, one of the clerks decided to break into his rooms, but, of course, the man had gone. All that was left behind was a rather grubby, blood-stained towel and a half-empty bottle of gin. What does that tell you about the man?'

'That is indeed a story,' smiled Ravenscroft, unsure whether he should question the young man further about this matter, but then deciding that the whole tale was probably a figment of Muncaster's over-active imagination.

'Ah, here we are,' announced Muncaster, stopping outside a tall Georgian building. 'If you would care to follow me, we should find Gervase on the next floor.'

Ravenscroft followed the young lawyer up the narrow flight of stairs until they reached the landing above, where Muncaster knocked loudly on the door facing them.

'Come in!' answered a voice Ravenscroft recognized.

'Gent to see you, Mr Webster,' said Muncaster gently opening the door.

'Ravenscroft,' said Webster, looking up from behind a partners' desk.

'Good day to you. I trust you received my telegram, Mr Webster. I was not in possession of your precise address,' said Ravenscroft, stepping into the room.

'Yes, but it is damned inconvenient. I am due in court in thirty minutes,' replied Webster, consulting a gold pocket watch.

'I shall not take up too much of your time, I can assure you.'

'All right I can give you ten minutes,' said Webster, in an irritated tone of voice. 'Well, you had better take a chair. Thank you, Mr Muncaster, you may go now.'

'Yes, Mr Webster. Good day to you, Mr Ravenscroft. It has been a pleasure to meet you. Perhaps one day our paths will cross again,' smiled Muncaster, as he closed the door behind him. Ravenscroft seated himself before the desk.

'I take it you have no news of my cousin?' said Webster.

'No. I am afraid not, but we have now been able to identify the dead man. Apparently he was a young teacher by the name of John Smith. His burial is due to take place tomorrow morning. We believe he trained as a barrister here in London. You might have heard of him?'

'John Smith you say? A common enough name, but it means nothing to me. The only John Smith I know was sentenced to five years' hard labour for defrauding an old widow out of her life savings, but that was twenty years ago, and the man was over fifty then.'

'He taught at a local school near Bromyard, called Glenforest. The principal is a man called Horace Smeaton.'

'The school is unknown to me, and I have certainly never heard of this Smeaton,' replied the lawyer, taking up his pen and signing some papers that lay on the desk.

'It would seem that your cousin, Miss Cleaves, visited the school about a month ago to see if it would be suitable to sponsor some boys from the village to attend there as pupils. She might have seen Mr Smith there,' suggested Ravenscroft.

'I would not know,' answered Webster without looking up.

'Could you tell me more about your cousin, Mr Cleaves's financial affairs?' asked Ravenscroft, wondering whether the lawyer would be forthcoming on this matter.

'I certainly cannot, sir,' said Webster finally looking up and glaring at Ravenscroft. 'Furthermore I consider it a gross impertinence on your part to ask such a question.'

'If we are to arrive at a solution to this mystery, and if I am to find the whereabouts of your cousin, it is imperative that I make these inquiries,' stressed Ravenscroft.

'I am Simon's cousin and legal adviser. What Simon has told me is an entirely confidential matter between these two walls. As a member of the police force I am sure that you understand that, Mr Ravenscroft.'

'It would still be of great value to us if we were to try and establish why your cousin left home, and where he could possibly be now,' persisted Ravenscroft, determined not to be put off by the barrister's forthright manner.

'And I have told you that I do not know of the whereabouts of my cousin, and that even if I did, I would certainly not impart that information to you. Now, if you will excuse me, this has taken up too much of my time. I must ask you to leave as I am awaited in court,' said Webster gathering up his papers, and indicating that the interview was at an end.

Ravenscroft knew that he had failed in his mission, and that he could no longer hope to obtain further information from the lawyer, but nevertheless he decided to attempt one further line of questioning. 'I have to tell you, Mr Webster, that we have interviewed your cousin, Miss Cleaves, and that we have been far from satisfied with the answers she has given us. I believe she is concealing valuable information about this case. It is my intention to arrest her tomorrow and take her in for further questioning.'

'That would be unwise, Inspector. Should I learn that you have, in any way, placed my cousin under any duress, or that you intend harassing her, then I warn you that you will have to answer to me. I trust that I have made myself clear on that point?' said Webster, his voice rising.

The two men stared at one another across the large desk.

'Good day to you, Mr Webster. I thank you for your assistance,' said Ravenscroft, walking out of the office and closing the door behind him.

* * *

An hour later he found himself in another part of London, entering a small office at the front of Bart's Hospital.

'Do please take a seat, Mr Ravenscroft,' said the distinguished, grey-haired, medical practitioner. 'You say that this is a police matter?'

'Yes, Dr Renshaw. I am presently undertaking an investigation into the death of a young man in the town of Upton-upon-Severn in Worcestershire.'

'And you believe that this man was a patient here at one time?'

'No. I am more interested in a Dr Stapleford, who conducted the medical examination of the dead man. I sent you a telegram earlier this week,' said Ravenscroft hopefully.

'Ah yes. I remember. You must excuse my negligence in not replying, but, as I am sure you must appreciate, we can sometimes be very busy here at Bart's,' said Renshaw, searching through a pile of correspondence on his desk.

'I understand that Dr Stapleford was engaged as a surgeon here for some years.'

'That was indeed so. Ah, here we are! I have your missive to hand, Inspector,' said the doctor, adjusting his pince-nez and reading the page intently.

'I was hoping that you would be able to tell me more about the doctor's activities during his time here.'

'That would be confidential information which I am not at liberty to divulge,' protested Renshaw, looking up and staring hard at Ravenscroft.

'I appreciate that, sir, but I am investigating a serious crime and I have to tell you that Dr Stapleford has come under suspicion,' said Ravenscroft firmly.

'I see,' said Renshaw placing his hands together and thinking deeply.

'Doctor Stapleford has an unusually large number of medical specimens in his house. Can you tell me whether he obtained them during his time here?' continued Ravenscroft determined to press on with his inquiries.

'We do keep some anatomical specimens here certainly, for medical research of course. I believe that Dr Stapleford may even have contributed to the collection.'

'But he did not collect specimens on his own account?'

Renshaw remained silent as he leaned back in his chair.

'It is a matter of great importance. Doctor Stapleford has come under police suspicion, as I have said,' emphasized Ravenscroft.

'What I have to tell you, Inspector, must remain in the strictest confidence,' said Renshaw after a few moments of silence had elapsed. 'This is quite difficult. Five years ago certain allegations were made by a number of our junior doctors here concerning Dr Stapleford.'

'Please go on, Doctor.'

'It was said that certain anatomical specimens had been removed from the laboratory by him for his own personal study and research, specimens which had not been returned to our collection. Upon further investigation it was also revealed that Stapleford removed vital organs from one or two patients, who . . . well, might have recovered from their operations. Conjecture, of course.'

'I see!' exclaimed Ravenscroft.

'Two of the board members and I felt obliged to conduct an internal investigation. We interviewed Stapleford, who denied all the accusations, and nothing was entirely proven, but it was felt that it would be better for the hospital if Stapleford resigned his position. It is very important that we retain the goodwill and support of our patrons, at all times, in the work that we undertake here. It is all a question of confidence, as I am sure you will appreciate. Any hint of scandal could possibly lead to the withholding of valuable funds and the ultimate closure of the hospital.'

'This is all most interesting, Dr Renshaw,' said Ravenscroft, relieved that at last he had obtained the truth concerning Stapleford. 'How long had he worked here?'

'For nearly twenty years. It was the end of a brilliant career. In exchange for Stapleford's silence it was agreed that he would receive a one-off gratuity and that he would leave with an unblemished record.'

'Can you tell me how he acquired the scar down the side of his face?' asked Ravenscroft.

'Apparently he obtained the injury during a particularly nasty disagreement with one of our porters some years ago. Doctor Stapleford was renowned for the shortness of his temper, but in this case it was thought that he had been severely provoked. The porter was, of course, instantly dismissed.'

'I see.'

'I hope all this has been of some assistance to you, Inspector? I'm afraid I cannot tell you anything else, and if you excuse me, I am awaited in theatre,' said Renshaw rising from his seat.

'Yes, of course, Doctor. You have been of great service to me.'

'I must stress, Inspector, that what I have told you today has been in the utmost confidence. Nothing of what you have learned in this room must be made public. The position and integrity of the hospital must be preserved at all times,' said Renshaw looking intently once more at Ravenscroft.

'Of course. I thank you again.'

CHAPTER FIVE

UPTON-UPON-SEVERN AND LUDLOW

'So there you have it, Tom, the result of my enquiries in London yesterday,' said Ravenscroft leaning back in his chair.

The two men were sitting in the inner office of the police station in Upton, the following morning.

'I always knew that Stapleford was a nasty character, all those body parts in glass jars. It's not natural,' replied Crabb.

'Yes, I am inclined to agree with you, and it may be that Stapleford is still intent on adding to his collection, but it may be difficult for us to prove that he is involved in any illegal activities. I wonder how many patients he has attended to in Upton since his arrival.'

'Not many by all accounts. Most of the local people in the town call on Dr Anderson. Stapleford was apparently only called out to examine the dead man because Anderson was away at the time.'

'Of course all this does not mean that Stapleford is involved in either the death of the schoolteacher Smith, or the disappearance of Simon Cleaves — and speaking of Cleaves, I gather there is still no information about the missing landowner?'

'No, sir, but Stapleford would certainly go to the top of my list of suspects,' added Crabb.

'It was rather frustrating that I was not able to obtain more information from Gervase Webster. He disclosed nothing and was quite hostile to my questions. We thought he would be intent on preserving the secrets of the family. I believe the time has now come to bring in Miss Cleaves for further questioning. I am convinced that she knows where her brother is and, until we have found him, we won't get to the bottom of this mystery. While in London I also took the liberty of calling on one or two of my old colleagues at the Yard to see if they had any information regarding the man Smith, but I am afraid they had no recollection of him. Oh, I was nearly forgetting, how did your investigations proceed in Bromyard yesterday?'

'I am afraid that there is little to relate sir. It seems that Smith never went into the town, so he was not in the habit of drinking in the inns there, and there certainly have been no reports of any strangers in the area with whom he might have arranged to meet.'

'So our mystery man keeps his secrets. What about the school?'

'As the school is situated on the Downs some two miles or so from the town, there appears to be little contact between the two. Smeaton visits the local bank occasionally, and the school cook comes into the town on a Friday to order fresh provisions. One or two of the local traders deliver to the school, and some of the boys occasionally attend church on a Sunday, but otherwise the school keeps very much to itself. There are the usual jests about rich boys getting above their station in life, but I could find no hint of any scandal. Apparently the school has been there for about ten years; the building was formerly used as an old workhouse and was even enlarged for that purpose some forty or so years ago. That is all I can tell you,' said Crabb closing his pocket book.

'I am not surprised it was a former workhouse. The whole place had a quite unfriendly and forbidding atmosphere about it. Mrs Ravenscroft was far from impressed. And I presume that Hoskings has obtained no further information here in Upton regarding the deceased man?'

'No, sir.'

'Do we know at what time Smith is to be buried?' asked Ravenscroft.

'In about thirty minutes, I believe.'

'Then we should certainly attend. I do not expect there will be many people at the interment, but it would be good to be seen to pay our respects, and I suppose there is always the remote possibility that Smith's murderer, if he was in fact murdered, might also attend.'

'Where is that blackguard Ravenscroft!' shouted a voice the detective recognized, from within the outer office.

Ravenscroft rose to his feet as the door was suddenly thrown open and an angry Stapleford stormed into the room.

'I am sorry, sir, I told the gentleman that you were busy, but he would not wait,' stuttered Hoskings alarmed.

'That is all right, Hoskings,' said Ravenscroft. 'What can I do for you, Dr Stapleford?

'What the blazes do you mean going behind my back consulting with my former colleagues at Bart's? Delving into my past!' growled Stapleford growing red in the face.

'Will you take a seat, Doctor?' answered Ravenscroft in a calm voice, hoping to placate the arrival's anger.

'No, sir, I will not! Just answer my question, man!'

'As we now believe the dead man most probably died as the result of a blow on the back of his head, administered by someone unknown—'

'Damn it, man! You think me a suspect? You think that I killed this man?' interrupted Stapleford.

'No, sir,' answered a flustered Ravenscroft. 'But as a police officer it is my duty to look into all possible avenues.'

'The blazes it is, man! How can I be a suspect? I was requested by your officer to make an examination of the body. I have never seen the man before, you idiot!' snarled Stapleford.

'You might be interested to know that we have identified the man as a certain John Smith. He was a schoolteacher at Glenforest School near Bromyard.'

'I tell you I have never heard of, or ever seen this man — and as for the Glenwhat's it place, I have never been anywhere near it! And as for that man, it is plain to everyone to see that he died as the result of a fall from his horse. Now what do you mean by sneaking off to Bart's and making yourself a nuisance there?' continued Stapleford, raising his stick and brandishing it at the detective.

'It is my duty to investigate everyone who is involved with this case,' replied Ravenscroft growing more unsettled, and wondering whether Stapleford was about to strike him.

'Nonsense! Confound you, sir! I will have satisfaction from you! I will sue you for every penny you have. I call this defamation of character. I have instructed my lawyer, Mr Sefton Rawlinson of the Inner Temple in London, to write to you, sir. You have not heard the last of it.'

'That is your prerogative, Dr Stapleford,' replied Ravenscroft positively wincing at the mention of the name of the great advocate.

'You are finished, Ravenscroft. Finished, I tell you. I will have satisfaction, I tell you. Good day to you, sir,' shouted Stapleford, as he marched out of the room, slamming the door loudly behind him.

'Well, he was certainly angry,' remarked Ravenscroft.

'I thought he was about to strike you at any moment,' said Crabb.

'So did I, Tom. Damn it! Someone at Bart's must have heard my conversation with Dr Renshaw yesterday and informed Stapleford. It seems as though he must still have friends there. The last thing I want now is that legal pomposity Sefton Rawlinson breathing down my neck,' sighed Ravenscroft.

'I think he means to ruin you, sir.'

'Then we had better find some evidence we can use against him as soon as possible,' sighed Ravenscroft. 'But enough of all this nonsense, we have a funeral to attend.'

* * *

As Ravenscroft and Crabb neared the burial ground they saw the empty hearse waiting at the side of the road.

'It seems as though Shortcross and Maudlin are here before us. They must be in somewhat of a hurry to bury the poor man,' said Ravenscroft.

'At least it is to be hoped that they have the right body this time,' added Crabb.

The two men walked up the path and were met by the three black-suited undertakers walking in solemn procession in the other direction.

'Good morning to you, gentlemen,' said Ravenscroft.

'Good morning to you, Inspector,' replied Reuben Thexton casting an uneasy glance at his two brothers.

'Have you buried Mr Smith already?' enquired Ravenscroft.

'We have indeed; the vicar was anxious to proceed as soon as possible. In view of the possibility of inclement weather,' offered Benjamin.

'Death waits for no one,' muttered Crabb.

'Tell me, gentlemen, did anyone attend the funeral?' asked Ravenscroft.

'Only the other gentleman, Mr Choke,' answered Reuben.

'There was no one else?'

'No, sir.'

'Then I wish you good day,' said Ravenscroft.

'The Lord is with him now,' pronounced Reuben making the sign of the cross and bowing his head as he passed by the two policemen.

'He is in Abraham's breast,' said Simeon Thexton with great solemnity.

'Amen, Brothers,' added Benjamin.

Ravenscroft and Crabb continued onwards and saw the lone figure of Marcus Choke, the schoolteacher, standing with bowed head before the open grave.

'Good morning, Mr Choke. This is a sad day,' said Ravenscroft somewhat at a loss for words.

'Poor John, do you know that I know neither his age, nor even his date of birth to put on his stone? What kind of legacy is that, Inspector?'

'At least you were here today, and he has been given a proper Christian burial. You could not have done more,' said Ravenscroft, seeking to give some kind of reassurance to the unhappy teacher.

'Our existence on this earth can be so fragile, Inspector. You work side by side every day, with someone, and then they are gone, taken from us so unexpectedly, like a butterfly that flies away and is seen no more. Life and death are so intertwined.'

'Indeed so,' replied Ravenscroft.

'All those months and he never told me the names of any of his relatives or friends. He must have been quite alone in this world,' continued Choke, mournfully.

'He would no doubt have been pleased by your presence, my dear Mr Choke. At least he had one friend, and you may yet be able to choose some appropriate words to be placed on his stone.'

'Yes. I must think of something suitable,' sighed Choke.

'We will leave you to your thoughts,' said Ravenscroft, about to take his leave.

'Have you been able to find out anything more about poor John, and why he left the school so suddenly?'

'I am afraid not, but our investigations are continuing, and you may rest assured that we will keep you informed.'

'Oh, I nearly forgot. It seems that John received a letter on the Friday morning before he disappeared.'

'Why was this not mentioned earlier?' asked Ravenscroft, anxious to know more.

'It was only when the other letter arrived this morning that the housekeeper remembered the first one,' said Choke.

'What other letter?'

'I have it here,' said Choke, reaching into his coat pocket. 'I was going to take it to the police station here in Upton after the service. It is addressed to John. I have not opened, it of course.'

Ravenscroft took the envelope. 'The franking is smudged, so we cannot see from where, and when, it was posted.'

'I trust it may be of importance,' said a concerned Choke.

Ravenscroft opened the envelope carefully, and began to read:

The Feathers Hotel
Ludlow
Thursday, 5 o'clock

My dearest John,

Why have I not heard from you? Why are you not here with me? Please come as soon as possible. My heart yearns to see you again. I am staying here at the Feathers in Ludlow. Can you be with me later today?

Your ever loving,
Rosemary

'Well that is interesting.'

'Short and to the point,' added Crabb.

'It would seem that this Rosemary must have been unaware that Smith was already dead when she wrote her letter,' said Ravenscroft, deep in thought.

'Oh dear,' said Choke. 'The poor woman. Whatever will she say when she learns of poor Mr Smith's death?'

'Perhaps it was also this lady who wrote the first letter?' suggested Crabb.

'Yes, and perhaps it was that letter which encouraged Smith to leave Glenforest so suddenly,' added Ravenscroft. 'I do not suppose you have this first letter as well?'

'No. John must have taken possession of it.'

'It is of no matter.'

'I hope I have done right, Mr Ravenscroft, in bringing you this letter?' asked Choke.

'Indeed you have, Mr Choke. This letter may well prove most valuable in our investigations.'

'May I ask what you will do now?' asked Choke.

'We must travel to Ludlow without delay and see if we can find this woman. She may be the answer to this mystery. We can travel from Malvern by train, I have no doubt, but first we must return to the office and consult Bradshaw. Thank you once again, Mr Choke,' said Ravenscroft.

'I wish you success with your endeavours,' said Choke, forcing a brief smile.

* * *

It was past the hour of two when Ravenscroft and Crabb alighted from the railway carriage at Ludlow Station. Making their way out of the building, Crabb observed an old man who was sitting on one of the seats, smoking.

'Can you tell us the way to the Feathers, my man?' asked Crabb.

'I can,' replied the man looking down at the ground, before taking another pull on his pipe.

'Well?' enquired Crabb, after some moments of silence had elapsed.

'Ah well, that all depends on who is asking,' mumbled the other sullenly.

'The police; we are the police.'

'Oh,' replied the man with indifference, before spitting on the floor.

'Well, are you going to direct us to the Feathers, or not?' repeated Crabb growing more annoyed.

'I might; but then again I might not.'

'Come on, Tom, we are wasting our time with this fellow,' said Ravenscroft beginning to move away. 'We will find it ourselves.'

'Surly fellow,' mumbled Crabb.

'And if you was born under a three-penny planet you'd never be worth four pence,' the old man shouted, as the two policemen left the outside of the station.

'Let us hope that the rest of the locals are not of the same sour temperament as our friend there,' remarked Ravenscroft.

After walking up a steep hill, where the fine Georgian three-storey buildings stood side by side with earlier half-timbered residences and businesses, Ravenscroft and Crabb found that they were standing outside the imposing structure of the Feathers Hotel.

Ravenscroft pushed open the heavy wooden door and adjusted his eyes to the ill-lit interior.

'Good morning to you, gentlemen,' said a breezy young clerk with a flourish of his arm. 'And welcome to the Feathers. How can I assist you? Two single rooms for the night? Every comfort is catered for. I am afraid lunch has already been served, but I expect we can find some morsel to refresh the weary traveller.'

'No, we require neither rooms, nor refreshment at present,' replied Ravenscroft.

'Oh dear, that all sounds rather solemn,' mimicked the clerk pulling a glum face before reverting his exuberant persona.

'We are police officers investigating the death of a man in Upton-upon-Severn.'

'I say, don't quite know where that is, but it sounds watery. How can the Feathers be of assistance?' asked the perplexed receptionist.

'I would be obliged if you would read this letter,' said Ravenscroft, reaching into his pocket and passing over the sheet of paper to the man. 'This letter was sent from this establishment to the dead man.'

'Rather strong, isn't it? I would say the lady has more than a passing acquaintance with your gentleman,' said the young man reading the letter intently before handing it to back.

'Do you have any young ladies staying here at present who might possess the Christian name of Rosemary?'

'No, I believe not,' replied the receptionist consulting a large ledger in front of him on the counter. 'Over half our rooms are occupied at present, mainly by commercial gentlemen. Ah, we do have two ladies staying with us, but they are quite well advanced in years. One is Lady Glendower. She must be seventy at least, and her aged companion must be even older. That would seem to be all.'

'Perhaps this lady was here yesterday, or even the day before?' suggested Crabb.

'No, there is no one here. I am sorry, but it appears that I cannot be of use to you,' replied the receptionist, closing the ledger with a bang.

'Could it be that a member of your staff wrote this letter,' asked a disappointed Ravenscroft. 'Perhaps a chambermaid, or scullery maid, might possess the name?'

'I cannot think that either Mavis or Ruth would have written such a letter,' laughed the man. 'The former is happily married with three children, and poor Ruth is, what you would say, rather on the large size and not of the brightest nature, so certainly not inclined to write such beguiling letters.'

'I see — and there is no one else?'

'I am afraid not, sir.'

'Thank you, my man,' sighed Ravenscroft.

'Do call upon us again should you ever find yourselves in Ludlow, gentlemen.'

'Well, sir, that was disappointing,' remarked Crabb, as the two men stood outside on the pavement.

'Most perplexing, I must say. I had hoped that we could have found this Rosemary and that she would have been able to enlighten us regarding the past history of John Smith. But why write such a letter, if you have no intention of being there? It doesn't make any sense.'

'What shall we do now?' asked Crabb.

'We must consider the possibility that this woman is to be found somewhere else in the town, so we will pay a visit to the local police station and see if they can throw any light on this matter, after which we may well have to go round all the other boarding establishments in the town in the hope that she is staying in one of those. I am determined at all costs, Tom, to find this woman, after how far we have come.'

* * *

Ravenscroft looked out at the dark sky from the carriage window of their train later that night, his mind occupied with the events of the day. First there had been the angry encounter with Stapleford in Upton, then Smith's funeral where Choke had revealed the letter which had been sent to the dead man, followed by their journey over to Ludlow to seek the mysterious 'Rosemary'. Here they had visited the Feathers Hotel, a quest which had proved futile. Then there had been the questioning of the local police officers in Ludlow which had added nothing to their investigations, and the long hours spent making inquiries in inns and boarding establishments in the town, all of which had failed to bring forth any information which might have led to a solution of the mystery. Now he and Crabb would be returning home after an empty day full of frustration and weariness; a day which could have been better spent in interrogating Anne Cleaves rather than in seeking out a woman who might, or might not, even have existed.

'Long day, sir,' remarked Crabb, reading his superior's thoughts, as the train pulled into Great Malvern Station.

'Yes. I think we will both be glad to get back to our respective firesides tonight,' said Ravenscroft opening the carriage door.

'Inspector! Inspector!' called out a familiar voice from further along the platform.

'It's Hoskings, sir,' said Crabb. 'He seems quite agitated about something.'

'Whatever is it that brings him out here at this time of the night? I pray there has been a development in the case.'

'Inspector Ravenscroft, terrible news, sir!' exclaimed a breathless Hoskings running up to meet them. 'It's absolutely terrible, sir.'

'Take your time Hoskings,' instructed Ravenscroft.

'We have just received news from Mathon Manor, sir. It is Miss Cleaves. She's dead! She has been murdered!'

CHAPTER SIX

MATHON MANOR

As Ravenscroft and Crabb alighted from the trap they were met by the anxious grey-haired butler.

'Mr Mansfield,' acknowledged Ravenscroft.

'Inspector, a terrible thing has occurred, sir.'

'I apologize for not arriving sooner. We have been in Ludlow for most of the day, and did not return until later this evening.'

'I understand, sir.'

'Before we go indoors, Mansfield, tell us what you know about this distressing situation.'

'Well, sir, Miss Cleaves retired to her room shortly after one this afternoon, saying that she was not to be disturbed on any account. At six this evening Charlotte, her personal maid, knocked on the bedroom door and, having received no reply, entered the room and found her mistress lying dead upon the bed. She immediately came downstairs and informed me of the situation. After confirming that Miss Cleaves was indeed dead, I locked the door to prevent other members of staff from entering, and then I sent the stable lad over to Upton to inform you of the situation. I have also summoned the doctor,' replied the butler, speaking in a quiet voice.

'Thank you, Mr Mansfield. You have acted quite correctly. Now, would you be so kind as to conduct us to Miss Cleaves's quarters.'

The two policemen followed the butler up the main staircase and along the landing, until they reached one of the bedrooms at the end of the passageway.

'It is all rather distressing, sir,' said Mansfield, his voice faltering as he unlocked the door.

'Most murders are,' replied Ravenscroft. 'We understand if you would prefer to remain here.'

'Thank you, sir, but I have served the family for over thirty years, and I feel that it is only right that I be with poor Miss Cleaves now in this hour of darkness.'

'I understand,' said Ravenscroft, opening the door and stepping into the room.

'Good Lord!' exclaimed Crabb looking towards the body which lay sprawled across the bed.

'Poor mistress,' said Mansfield.

'It would seem that Miss Cleaves has been strangled,' pronounced Ravenscroft after examining the corpse. 'There is a piece of ribbon which has been placed around her neck, which has then been tightly pulled. By the state of the sheets, I would say that she put up quite a struggle.'

'There is a window open over here, sir,' said Crabb.

'So you think our murderer could have entered that way? That could be so. I see that the top drawer of the bedside cabinet has been opened. Do we know what Miss Cleaves kept in here?'

'Some of her jewellery, sir,' replied Mansfield, preferring to stand by the door.

'Which now appears to have been taken,' said Crabb, peering into the empty drawer.

Ravenscroft crossed over to the window and leaned out over the edge. 'I don't think our intruder entered this way, unless he, or she, was a cat. It is quite a long way down to the ground, and although there appears to be some ivy growing over the walls, I don't believe it would have supported any great weight. We can confirm that tomorrow when we examine the outside of the house in daylight, but I would say that the killer left the window open on his departure to make us believe that an intruder had both entered and left that way. Mansfield, do we know if there have been any reports of any strangers recently arrived in the area?'

'I am not aware of any such reports, sir.'

'Did any of the servants notice any strange person in the grounds this afternoon?'

'No one has reported such an incident to me, but I will of course make further enquiries, if you so wish.'

'I would be obliged. Also, I would like to know whether anyone heard any strange sounds this afternoon. Miss Cleaves may have cried out before she was killed,' continued Ravenscroft.

'I will ask the servants, but I would have assumed that had the mistress cried out, the servants would have come to her aid.'

'I would like a word with Miss Cleaves's maid — Charlotte, I think you said,' said Ravenscroft.

'Of course, sir,' replied Mansfield, giving a short bow before leaving the room and closing the door behind him.

'Confound it, Crabb!' exclaimed Ravenscroft. 'If only we had come here this morning and taken Miss Cleaves into custody, as we intended, then the poor woman would have still been alive, but instead we wasted the whole day in that wretched town trying to find a woman who apparently does not exist.'

'We were not to know that at the time,' offered Crabb.

'Then we should have known. It was obvious that Miss Cleaves could have provided us with the solution to this mystery, and now it looks as though we have two murders to solve. This will not do at all, Tom,' said an agitated Ravenscroft.

'You don't think it was an intruder, some tramp or vagabond, who came in through the window?' asked Crabb, trying to turn his superior's thoughts away from his recriminations.

'No. I believe Miss Cleaves retired to her room, giving strict instructions that she was not to be disturbed, because she was expecting that someone would call upon her. The fact that some jewellery was taken, and the window left open, was a rather crude attempt by our murderer to make us believe that she had been killed by an opportunist burglar or intruder. Quickly, Tom, I can hear noises outside, let us cover the body over with this sheet before the maid enters,' instructed Ravenscroft.

A reluctant Crabb leant over the bed and assisted Ravenscroft with his task.

'Enter,' said Ravenscroft in response to a knock on the door.

'Charlotte, the maid, sir,' said Mansfield entering.

'You are Miss Cleaves's maid?' asked Ravenscroft, as the young woman came hesitantly into the room.

'Yes, sir,' replied the girl in a quiet, nervous tone of voice. Ravenscroft observed that she had been crying, and that she gave a brief, frightened glance towards the bed before looking down at her feet.

'There is nothing to be afraid of now, Charlotte,' said Ravenscroft trying to sound reassuring. 'We would like you to answer some questions for us, if you will?'

'Yes, sir.'

'How long have you been Miss Cleaves's personal maid?'

'For about five or six years. Before that I was one of the housemaids for two years.'

'We understand that your mistress retired to her room shortly after luncheon?'

'Yes, sir.'

'What time was that exactly?'

'It was about one o'clock, sir.'

'And what did she say to you? '

'That she had a headache, and that on no account was she to be disturbed before six o'clock,' replied the maid, still looking down at her feet.

'Tell me, Charlotte, were you surprised by your mistress's words?'

'Begging your pardon, sir, but I don't understand you,' said the maid looking up briefly at Ravenscroft, a puzzled expression on her face.

'Were you surprised by your mistress's instructions, or was Miss Cleaves in the habit of retiring to her room in the afternoons?'

'Mistress sometimes went to her room, after one, but she always came down for afternoon tea at four.'

'So you were surprised when she said she was not to be disturbed until after six?'

'Yes, sir.'

'And then you came up here, at what time?'

'It was just after six o'clock, sir?'

'And then?' prompted Ravenscroft.

'Well, I tapped on the door. Then when I received no answer I called out. I thought something must have happened to the mistress so I opened the door and saw . . .' continued the maid, her voice trailing away as tears again began to well up in her eyes.

'Don't distress yourself, girl. The inspector has to ask these questions if we are to catch the terrible person who did this deed,' said Mansfield, offering a handkerchief to the sobbing maid.

'Who can have done this terrible thing, sir?' asked Charlotte through her tears.

'We do not know at present, Charlotte, but you may rest assured that we will catch this evil person. In the meantime you can be of great assistance to us.'

'Me, sir? How can I be of help?'

'We believe a number of items may have been taken away from this room. We would be obliged if you would go through Miss Cleaves's personal effects and tell us whether anything has been removed,' smiled Ravenscroft, encouragingly.

'Yes, sir,' replied Charlotte, crossing over to the bedside cabinet.

Ravenscroft and Crabb remained silent as the maid went through the drawers.

'The mistress's jewellery has been taken. She kept it here in the top drawer.'

'Anything else?' enquired Ravenscroft.

'There is nothing else, sir.'

'Would you please look in the wardrobe, and then through Miss Cleaves's personal papers in her writing bureau?' instructed Ravenscroft.

'Yes, sir.'

'Mr Mansfield, has Lady Cleaves been informed of her niece's death?' asked Ravenscroft, as the maid carried out her task.

'Yes, sir. She has taken it rather badly, and has retired to her room for the night. I have instructed her maid to keep a watchful eye on her,' replied the butler.

'Very wise, Mansfield. I think it would also be advisable if Mr Webster was also informed of today's sad events.'

'I sent one of the servants to the telegraph office in Malvern earlier this evening.'

'Excellent. You seem to have thought of everything, Mansfield.'

'Please, sir,' interrupted the maid, 'I think some of the mistress's letters have been taken.'

'Can you elaborate?' asked Ravenscroft keenly.

'There was a bundle of letters which she kept in the top drawer of the bureau.'

'How many of these letters were there?'

'I think there were about ten or eleven letters, sir. Miss Cleaves tied them together with a pink ribbon.'

'I see. This is all very interesting, Charlotte. Did Miss Cleaves say who the letters were from?' asked Ravenscroft, anxious to know more.

'No, sir. She said nothing at all about them.'

'How long had she been receiving letters?'

'For about two or three months, sir.'

'Tell me, Charlotte, in your opinion, do you think these letters were from an admirer?' suggested Ravenscroft.

'I don't know, sir. Miss Cleaves never said, but she always seemed pleased when one of the letters arrived.'

'Did she reply to these letters?'

'I believe so, sir.'

'Would you happen to know the name of the person to whom her replies were sent?' continued Ravenscroft.

'No, sir. Miss Cleaves always posted her own letters, usually when she went into Malvern or Worcester, I believe.'

'That is very strange,' commented Ravenscroft.

'I know that Mr Simon wasn't very pleased,' added the maid.

'Oh, why do you say that?'

'There was one day, about three weeks ago, when the mistress received one of her letters, and he became very annoyed. They were sitting at the breakfast table at the time.'

'Do you remember what Mr Simon said upon that occasion?'

'He said something like "I suppose you have got another letter from that scoundrel", or words to that effect.'

'This is all most illuminating,' said Ravenscroft. 'Tell me, did your master ever say who this man was?'

'No, sir,'

'Thank you, Charlotte. You have been most helpful to us. Perhaps you would sit down with Mr Mansfield early tomorrow morning and make a list of Miss Cleaves's jewellery,' said Ravenscroft, disappointed that such a promising line of inquiry had come to an inconclusive end.

'Yes, sir. Can I go now?'

'Yes, Charlotte. Oh, there is just one more thing: can you tell me what you were doing this afternoon after your mistress retired to her room?'

'I helped Anne, the downstairs maid, to clean some of the silver in the drawing room for most of the afternoon. Why do you ask?'

'Am I correct in assuming that the drawing room opens out onto the front hall?'

'Yes sir.'

'So if anyone came into the house, through the front entrance, you would have seen or heard them.'

'Yes, sir, but there was no one.'

'Thank you, Charlotte. You may go. Thank you once again for answering our questions.'

The maid gave a short curtsy and left the room.

'Would that Mr Simon was here now in our hour of need,' Mansfield sighed. 'I suppose there is still no news?'

'I am sorry, Mr Mansfield.'

'I was here when both of them were born, you know. They were such pleasant children. I watched them both growing up. It is all so very sad, so very sad.'

'I am sure that Mr Cleaves will be found shortly. Can you tell me whether there is another way onto this landing; a back stairs perhaps?' asked Ravenscroft.

'Yes, sir. If you would both care to follow me, gentlemen.'

Ravenscroft and Crabb followed the butler out onto the landing.

'There is a flight of stairs at the end, which leads to the lower floor,' said Mansfield locking the bedroom door behind him.

'Please show us the way.'

The two detectives followed the butler down a flight of narrow, winding steps.

'As you can see, Inspector, we have arrived at the back of the house,' remarked Mansfield, as they reached the lower level. 'These stairs are generally only used by the servants.'

'And where does that door lead to?' asked Ravenscroft.

'The kitchens are through there, sir.'

'Could our intruder have entered the house that way?'

'He could, but he would have had to go through the kitchens and the scullery and, as the cook and the kitchen maid are usually in there, it would have been impossible not to have been seen by them.'

'And what is this door?'

'That leads to a store cupboard.'

'Is it usually kept unlocked?' continued Ravenscroft with his questioning.

'Yes.'

'May we enter?'

'Of course,' answered the butler opening the door.

Ravenscroft and Crabb entered the small dark room.

'We store all the laundry in here, and other household items,' said Mansfield.

'I would be obliged if you could hold the lamp high so that we can see around,' asked Ravenscroft.

'Of course, sir,' replied Mansfield, complying with the request.

'This window over here; I see that it has a catch on the inside,' said Ravenscroft, crossing over to the other side of the crowded room.

'Yes, sir. The window is usually locked.'

'Interesting, but I see that it is not engaged.'

'You don't think the man came in through the window?' asked a perplexed Mansfield.

'Hand me the lamp,' instructed Ravenscroft, ignoring the question as he raised the sash window upwards.

The butler passed over the lamp to Ravenscroft, who leaned out of the window. 'Ah, I see some rather indistinct marks on the ground down here, which may have been caused by a boot or shoe of some kind. Tell me what you think, Constable Crabb.'

'I am inclined to agree with you, sir,' said Crabb, after he had taken the lamp from Ravenscroft and peered down at the ground.

'To answer your question, Mr Mansfield, I think it is highly likely that this was the way our intruder entered and left the building this afternoon. Had he entered by either the front entrance, or through the kitchens, he would have certainly been seen by one or more of the servants,' pronounced Ravenscroft.

'Good heavens!' uttered the usually unflappable butler.

'Thank you for your attention, Mr Mansfield. I do not think there is anything else we can accomplish at this late hour. Whoever committed this terrible crime will no doubt be a long way from here by now. Constable Crabb and I will return in the morning to continue our investigations,' said Ravenscroft, closing the door to the linen room behind him.

'Of course, sir, I will show you both out,' said the butler leading the way down the corridor.

'Miss Cleaves dead you say, girl?' suddenly boomed out a loud voice, that Ravenscroft recognized, from the main hall.

'Good evening, Dr Stapleford,' said Mansfield addressing the medical man.

'Good evening to you, Mansfield. Good Lord! Ravenscroft, what the blazes are you doing here?' said the surprised doctor confronting the detective.

'You may recall, Doctor, that I am investigating the demise of the young man, John Smith, enquiries that have led me here. I came as soon I received the news of Miss Cleaves's death. This is a terrible business, Doctor,' said Ravenscroft trying to avoid looking at the new arrival.

'Damn inconvenient being called out at such a late hour. I suppose you had better lead the way, Mansfield,' grumbled Stapleford after throwing Ravenscroft a menacing glance.

'If you will follow me, sir,' said the butler leading the way up the stairs.

The two policemen stood for some moments in the hallway, watching the doctor disappear from view, before Ravenscroft spoke.

'Now what the devil has that man to do with the Cleaves family?'

CHAPTER SEVEN

MATHON AND UPTON-UPON-SEVERN

'You must not blame yourself, Samuel, for that poor woman's death,' said Lucy, attempting to break her husband's melancholic thoughts over breakfast on the following morning.

'But I do. I keep telling myself that if I had carried out my intention of questioning Anne Cleaves, instead of delaying things by going on that futile journey to Ludlow, she would still be alive,' replied the detective gloomily, before taking another sip of tea from his breakfast cup.

'You were not to know that. You believe that it was this man, her lover, who killed her?'

'I am sure of it. He must have instructed her to leave the laundry-room window open so that he could enter unobserved, and make his way up the stairs to her room. After he murdered the poor woman he took the letters, which obviously would have incriminated him, also stole the jewels and opened the bedroom window, in the hope that we would assume that an intruder had entered that way and committed the crime.'

'Who could possibly have done such a dreadful thing?'

'I wish I knew, but I do know that her murder must be linked to that of the death of the young schoolteacher at

Glenforest. Now I am more than ever convinced that Smith was murdered, and that he did not die as the result of a fall from his horse,' said Ravenscroft, removing his spectacles and polishing them on his napkin.

'I must say that this case must be one of your most baffling,' sympathized Lucy.

'Yes. First we have the disappearance of Simon Cleaves to investigate, then the apparent murder of John Smith in Upton last Saturday, and now we are faced with the death of that poor woman. I am sure that all three events are connected in some way, but I cannot see how. If only Cleaves would appear again, then he might be able to throw some light on this case, but until then we are working in the dark.'

'So what will you and Tom do today?' asked Lucy, pouring more tea into her husband's cup.

'Return to Mathon Court and make further inquiries. Someone might have just seen our murderer. I hope that Gervase Webster will have arrived, and that he will be more forthcoming concerning the affairs of the family, now that his cousin has been killed,' replied Ravenscroft, replacing his spectacles.

'I have been thinking about that school, Glenforest. We know that Anne Cleaves visited it, apparently with a view to sending local boys from the village there, and she must have met Mr Smith then?' suggested Lucy.

'Yes, that is a possibility I suppose, although both Choke and Smeaton say that the two never met. John Smith cannot have been Anne Cleaves's murderer, because he has already been dead a week. No, if we can only ascertain just who wrote those letters to Anne Cleaves then we will have our killer.'

'But why would her lover have killed her?' asked Lucy.

'To stop her telling us something important that must relate to Smith's death. Anne Cleaves probably knew who killed Smith and that was why she had to be killed.'

'Well, from what you have told me, it seems that her brother did not approve of her relationship with this man.'

'Yes. If only he had revealed who his sister's lover was, but then perhaps she never told him.'

'I don't like that doctor,' remarked Lucy, changing the direction of the conversation. 'The man is a bully, and has clearly been up to no good in the past. I am not surprised he was compelled to leave that hospital in London.'

'I must admit though that it was rather a shock when he walked into the house yesterday evening. Mansfield obviously sent for him because Stapleford has some association with the family. Interestingly, when we first interviewed Stapleford he claimed he had no knowledge of Simon Cleaves.'

'You don't think the evil doctor was Anne Cleaves's secret admirer?'

'You would not ask that question if you had ever met Stapleford. With that scar running down the side of his face, and his offensive, offhand manner, he would not hold any appeal for a woman.'

'Some members of my sex have been known to strike up romantic attachments with the most peculiar of men,' joked Lucy.

'I trust that you do not include yourself in their number?' smiled Ravenscroft.

'Excuse me, sir, a letter has just arrived for you,' said the maid, entering the room.

'Thank you, Susan,' said Ravenscroft, taking hold of the envelope. 'I don't recognize the handwriting. I see that it is sent from London. All looks very formal. . . The blazes! How dare the man!'

'Whatever is the matter?' asked a startled Lucy.

'It's from that mountebank, Sefton Rawlinson! It says that I have damaged the professional reputation of his client, Dr Stapleford, and that he is bringing a charge of defamation of character against me, unless I desist from any further contact with his client, and agree to pay the sum of one hundred and fifty pounds in damages!' exclaimed Ravenscroft, angrily throwing the paper down onto the table.

'The audacity of the man!' said a concerned Lucy. 'Whatever will you do, Samuel? We don't have that kind of money.'

'I will treat this letter with the contempt it deserves. I will never pay that man a penny. I would rather become a beggar in Whitechapel than give that man any kind of satisfaction. No. He will not get away with this!'

* * *

'Well, sir, you certainly seem to have made him angry,' said Crabb, after reading the letter in the police station in Upton.

'Am I never to be free from that man Rawlinson? I have faced him many times over the years at the Bailey, where he has always sought to pour scorn on my attempts to bring the villains of Whitechapel to book, but never has he stooped so low as to threaten me with this.'

'What will you do now?'

'Ignore the letter for the present and go on the offensive — or rather, Tom, you will,' replied Ravenscroft.

'How, sir?' asked Crabb, bewildered.

'I am sure there is a lot more to unearth regarding the activities of Stapleford here in Upton. I want you to question as many people here in the town as you can. Find out what people really think about him; have there been any rumours concerning his practice; how many patients has the doctor seen in the past; how many now is he administering medicines to, have any of them died in mysterious or unusual circumstances; all that kind of thing.'

'Leave it to me, sir. If there is any evidence against the man, I will find it,' said Crabb, trying to sound reassuring.

'Good man.'

'And where will you be, sir?'

'I will be returning to Mathon Manor. I want to know who killed Anne Cleaves.'

* * *

As Ravenscroft alighted from the trap, he noticed the familiar horse-drawn vehicle of the Upton undertakers positioned directly outside the main entrance of the house.

'Good day to you, Mr Thexton,' said Ravenscroft addressing the man whom he remembered as Simeon Thexton.

'Good day, Inspector. This is a sad day.'

'Indeed.'

'A young lady cut down in her prime,' replied Simeon mournfully, shaking his head.

The main doors of the house opened and a group of servants, including Mansfield and the maid Charlotte, came out onto the steps and lined up on either side of the entrance. Ravenscroft observed that several of the maids had been crying, and that Mansfield had given a brief nod of recognition in his direction. Then, the aged figure of Lady Cleaves, joined the others, her face covered by a tight black veil, one hand clutching a walking stick, her other arm supported by one of the servants.

'Brothers and Sisters, in the midst of life we are in death,' intoned the voice of Reuben Thexton as he made his way down the steps, followed by a coffin borne by his brother Benjamin, and three of the male servants.

'Amen,' echoed Simeon, opening the back partition of the covered wagon.

'Gently, Brothers,' instructed Reuben, as the coffin was placed on the back of the cart and slid forward into position.

'She is in the Lord's hands now,' cried out Benjamin.

'Indeed she is, Brother Benjamin,' said Simeon.

'The good Lord will be with her always,' added Reuben taking his place behind the horse.

'The Lord will bless her and keep her safe in His company,' continued Benjamin, bowing before the coffin, before replacing his black top hat and taking his place on the wagon.

'She is with the angels now. The Lord bless us all and keep us in His heart,' said Benjamin Thexton, making a sign of the cross before joining his two brothers.

Ravenscroft watched motionless, as the wagon turned away from the building and made its slow dignified progress down the drive, between the rows of trees, until it disappeared from view. Then he looked up at the darkening sky, as a wave of despair and recrimination seemed about to overwhelm him.

Anne Cleaves had left her home for the last time.

'Now then, we must all attend to our duties,' said Mansfield, breaking the silence and addressing the servants, as Lady Cleaves made her way slowly back into the building.

'Good day to you, Mr Mansfield,' said Ravenscroft, as the servants dispersed, and the butler came forward to meet him.

'Good day to you, Inspector, although I do not believe that we can call it such,' remarked the butler solemnly.

'Lady Cleaves must have found it particularly difficult,' stuttered Ravenscroft, unsure of what to say.

'As indeed we all do. I had never thought that I would see this day.'

'Indeed not.'

'I suppose there is no news of Mr Simon?'

'I am afraid not.'

'I have the list of the mistress's missing jewellery,' continued Mansfield, handing a piece of paper to the detective.

'Thank you, Mansfield,' replied Ravenscroft briefly, looking at its contents before placing the paper in his pocket. 'I take it that Mr Webster has not arrived yet?'

'No, sir. We have received no communication from the gentleman. I have taken the liberty of interviewing all the servants and farm hands, to see if any of them saw anyone or anything unusual in the vicinity of the house yesterday, but it appears that no one saw anything out of the ordinary.'

'Thank you, Mansfield. I would like to look round the house and grounds on my own now, if I may?'

'Of course, sir, please feel free to do so.'

'Perhaps you would be kind enough to inform me when Mr Webster arrives.'

'Yes, sir.'

'Oh, there is one more thing: Last night. Doctor Stapleford. Can you tell me what connection he has with the family?' enquired Ravenscroft.

'He has been in attendance to both Lady Cleaves and Miss Anne for the past six months, I believe.'

'I see — and was he a frequent visitor here?'

'Not at first, but during the last three or four months I would say that he has visited the house every two or three weeks.'

'This was to see Lady Cleaves, I presume?'

'Oh no, sir, it was Miss Anne that he came to visit.'

'That is most interesting. I don't suppose you know what ailed Miss Cleaves?' probed Ravenscroft.

'I am afraid not, sir. Miss Cleaves confided in no one. The consultations, or treatments, usually lasted only a few minutes, and were sometimes conducted in Miss Cleaves's bedroom.'

'Was Miss Cleaves's maid in attendance during these treatments?'

'I believe not, sir.'

'Do not you find that somewhat unusual?'

'Whatever the reason for her consultation, she did not confide in the servants.'

'Did you notice that Miss Cleaves had been unwell?'

'No, sir. She seemed quite healthy to me, although perhaps a little pale of complexion of late. I expect it was the anxiety concerning her brother's absence.'

'Thank you, Mansfield.'

Ravenscroft entered the house and made his way up the stairs and entered Anne Cleaves's bedroom. The room seemed to have taken on a cold, quiet aspect now that its owner had given up its residence. He observed that someone had made a half-hearted attempt to straighten the sheets on the bed, and that the smell of death, which he had long come to recognize in such situations, hung loosely in the air.

After going through the drawers in the bedside cabinet once again, and examining the many dresses in the wardrobe,

Ravenscroft turned his attention first to the writing bureau and then the several volumes that lay on the small set of shelves at its side, but after some minutes he realized that he had found nothing of interest. Next he knelt down on the floor and looked under the bed, before turning back the sheets and examining beneath the mattress. Then he looked around the room for some moments, deep in thought, before finally studying the carpet to see if any vital evidence could be found there.

Ravenscroft sighed as he closed the bedroom door behind him. He carefully made his way along the corridor and down the wooden winding stairs, his eyes continually focused on the floor and steps, until his journey brought him once again to the laundry room. Opening the door, he entered and after a quick examination of the shelves upon which the neat piles of linen were stacked he crossed over to the window. He moved the catch and lifted up the sash, and lowered himself through the open space onto the garden outside. He examined the ground directly beneath the window where he had noticed the disturbed earth from the previous evening.

Looking up and seeing a path leading into a wood situated a few yards from the house, Ravenscroft soon found himself following its course into the dark interior. Brushing his way past the overhanging branches he found that the wood eventually opened out into a small clearing where he observed that the undergrowth showed signs of having been recently disturbed. Again he followed the path and found himself standing in a small lane on the other side of the wood, and realized that in all probability this was the way the intruder had used to enter and leave the building, and why he had been able to do so without detection. But although his journey had confirmed his suspicions, he was also acutely aware that the man had left nothing behind to incriminate him, and that he was still far away from establishing the killer's identity.

Retracing his steps through the wood, and back through the window, Ravenscroft closed the door of the linen room behind him, and made his way back to the front hall.

'I say, what an absolutely marvellous place!' exclaimed a voice that Ravenscroft instantly recognized.

'Timothy Muncaster!' cried out Ravenscroft.

'Good Lord, if it is not Ravenscroft again. Well I'll be darned,' smiled the new arrival.

'Whatever brings you to Mathon Manor?' asked Ravenscroft perplexed.

'Mr Webster. When he got the telegram, he realized he could not come down straight away. He is involved in some big fraud case at the Bailey. So he asked me if I could come down here and hold the fort until he arrived. Although I must admit that I don't quite know what I am supposed to do. Pay my respects to the old lady, I suppose, and adopt a mournful face.'

'Well, I am sure that your presence here will be much appreciated,' said Ravenscroft.

'I will have your luggage taken up to your room, sir,' said Mansfield casting a wary look in the young man's direction. 'Perhaps you would care for some tea in the drawing room?'

'Tea? I've had enough tea in the Temple to last me a lifetime. Wouldn't say no to something stronger though,' replied Muncaster.

'Perhaps I could take Mr Muncaster into the drawing room and offer him some liquid refreshment?' suggested Ravenscroft.

'Indeed, sir.'

'Come this way, Muncaster,' said Ravenscroft.

'I say, this place gets better and better,' said the young lawyer staring all around him. 'They must be worth a few sovereigns these Cleaves people. Old Gervase kept quiet about all this.'

'Take a seat. I will see what I can find,' suggested Ravenscroft, exploring the contents of a large silver tray. 'Would whisky be all right?'

'More than all right, I'd say. Perfect, my dear sir,' said Muncaster almost throwing himself onto the large sofa.

'I must say that I am somewhat relieved by your presence here,' said Ravenscroft, handing the lawyer a glass.

'Glad to be of service. I take it the case is not going well then?'

'I don't know what Webster has told you regarding the telegram he received,' began Ravenscroft, seating himself in one of the large armchairs.

'He said only that Miss Cleaves had been murdered, and that they would be obliged if he could come down here as soon as possible. It all sounds quite a nasty business. I told you that these kind of unpleasant things always happened in the country.'

'You did indeed,' smiled Ravenscroft.

'Any suspects lined up yet?' enquired Muncaster.

'Not at the present.'

'And where did this terrible act take place?'

'The poor lady was murdered in her bedroom yesterday afternoon. It seems that the intruder made his way in through a downstairs window,' replied Ravenscroft, realizing that he was perhaps letting the young man know more than he was entitled to.

'What a terrible state of affairs.'

'Anyway, our investigations are proceeding, and I am confident that we shall apprehend the killer eventually. I don't suppose Mr Webster ever mentioned to you anything concerning the affairs of the family?'

'Good Lord, no. Gervase is a canny fellow. He keeps his affairs and his thoughts very much to himself. Sorry, can't help.'

'Actually there is something on which I would be glad of your opinion,' said Ravenscroft, reaching into his pocket. 'I received this today.'

Muncaster took it and read the contents of the letter. 'I say, this is a damned cheek!'

'That's what I thought.'

'The great Sefton Rawlinson, no less.'

'You know of the gentleman?'

'Everyone in the Temple knows of Sefton Rawlinson. He is a particular slithery customer in all respects!'

'I encountered him a number of times during my career in Whitechapel.'

'Then you have my profound sympathies, my dear sir. Sefton Rawlinson is a barrister we young fellows seek to avoid as much as possible. To come up against that colossus could well result in the total eclipse of one's career before it has even begun! I take it that this Dr Stapleford is one of the suspects in the case that you mentioned. Someone called Smith? You showed me his photograph I believe,' replied Muncaster, leaning forwards, and showing a keen interest.

'Yes, he was a schoolmaster at one of the local schools. I would be glad of your professional opinion regarding the letter.'

'It is all puff and bravado, my dear sir; puff and bravado! Of course I could take on your case, beard the lion in his den and all that, but we might come out the wrong side. My professional advice would be fold it up in one's pocket and forget all about it for a while.'

'I am not sure that would be prudent.'

'Tell you what I'd do: I'll draft out a suitable reply, delaying tactics and all that, while admitting nothing. No commitment on your part. Give you time to press home your advantage. Let you see it before dispatch,' said Muncaster enthusiastically.

'That would be much appreciated,' replied Ravenscroft.

The two men were disturbed by the sudden opening of the door.

'Lady Cleaves,' said Ravenscroft, as the two men rose quickly to their feet.

'I take it you have no news of my nephew Simon?'

'I am afraid not, Lady Cleaves. May I offer my sincere condolences for your sad loss,' said Ravenscroft, feeling awkward in the old woman's presence.

'Find him, Ravenscroft. Find him. We have a great need for him in this our hour of need.'

'Of course, Lady Cleaves, I can assure you that everything is being done. We have the police forces of the Three Counties making detailed searches.'

Lady Cleaves gave Ravenscroft a look of cold disbelief, before turning to face Muncaster. 'And who are you, sir?'

'I am Timothy Muncaster, at your service, Lady Cleaves.'

'And what is it that you do, Mr Muncaster?'

'I am a barrister in the Temple in London. Gervase, er Mr Webster, is a good friend of mine. He has asked me to convey his respects to your ladyship, and to tell you that he hopes to be here later tonight. He is unfortunately delayed on business. Big fraud case at the Bailey and all that,' replied a somewhat deflated Muncaster, his voice trailing off to an almost inaudible whisper.

'If you will excuse me, Lady Cleaves, I must continue with this investigation,' said Ravenscroft, anxious to leave the room as soon as possible. 'Muncaster, a good day to you.'

Lady Cleaves did not look in Ravenscroft's direction and, as he left the room, he thought he saw the helpless Muncaster give him a look of desperation as the young barrister shuffled his feet before the elder's presence.

* * *

As Ravenscroft's trap made its way in Upton later that afternoon, the detective turned up the collar of his coat as the threatening clouds above finally began to discharge their contents.

He had spent several hours at Mathon Manor that day, interviewing the servants, stable lads, and farmhands, but had gained no fresh information. Then he had visited the village itself, and had even extended his inquiries to nearby Colwall but no one there had any recollection of having seen a stranger in the vicinity the previous afternoon. The killer had been very careful, concealing both his arrival and his departure in the area from anyone who might have later provided a description of his appearance. Now it was a weary Ravenscroft who was returning to the police station, hoping that Crabb had been more fortunate than himself in his investigations, or that there had been some important developments in the case during his absence.

'Crabb. Hoskings,' said Ravenscroft walking quickly into the station. 'What news?'

'Well, sir, at around eleven o'clock this morning the Thexton brothers arrived in the town with Miss Cleaves's body. I saw them carrying the coffin into their premises,' replied Crabb taking out his pocket book.

'Yes, I was there at Mathon Manor when they took the poor girl away. It was a very sad occasion. Go on.'

'Well, just as I was turning away from the place I saw that manservant Parsons, the one we encountered at Stapleford's residence when we visited there. He went into the undertaker's building and emerged shortly afterwards. I was careful to see that he did not observe my presence.'

'Now that is interesting. I wonder what he was doing at the Thextons' premises?'

'Hoskings and I have also interviewed practically the whole town. Hardly anyone is, or has, been a patient of Dr Stapleford. It is not just that he is regarded as something of a recluse, more that the local doctor has been here for over twenty years or more and has built up an established practice. However, I did find out that two of Stapleford's patients had died within the past year. The first was a young boy of thirteen years or so, an Oliver Thompson, who had a deformed spine. The second patient was a young girl, Sally Owens, who had a bad cough. I interviewed both sets of parents, and they both said that their children had both died unexpectedly while being treated by Stapleford.'

'This is all very intriguing, Crabb,' said Ravenscroft, enthusiastic to know more.

'I had words with the local registrar of Births, Deaths and Marriages, who let me see copies of the death certificates. Both had been signed by Stapleford, and both entries gave the cause of death as "sudden heart failure brought on by existing medical conditions".'

'Go on.'

'There is more, sir. It seems that both Sally Owens and this Oliver Thompson were buried in the local burial ground.

I was able to locate their burial plots. Fortunately the local gravedigger was present at the site, and he told me something quite interesting. Apparently, two or three days after Sally Owens was interred the gravedigger entered the graveyard in the morning and noticed that the earth on top of her burial plot was freshly disturbed. Likewise when young Thompson died there were also signs that the earth was disturbed in a likewise fashion.'

'Why on earth did the man not report this matter to the authorities at the time?' asked Ravenscroft.

'Well, apparently, he just thought that the relatives had visited the graves and had disturbed the earth during their mourning.'

'Well done, Tom. This is just what we have been looking for,' said Ravenscroft, relieved.

'You don't think—' began Crabb.

'That Stapleford deliberately killed his two young patients then removed their bodies from the burial ground, so that he could use them for his medical research?'

'Good Lord!' exclaimed Hoskings, looking somewhat stunned.

'I wouldn't put it past him, sir,' agreed Crabb. 'He is a nasty character.'

'Yes, but how are we to prove that this was the case?'

'We could exhume the bodies to see if they are still in their coffins?'

'We would need very good evidence in order to proceed with such a course of action,' said Ravenscroft, deep in thought.

'Or we could just go along to the graveyard tonight and dig them up ourselves?' suggested Hoskings.

'I don't think I heard that remark, Constable. Of course, Anne Cleaves!' suddenly exclaimed Ravenscroft.

'Anne Cleaves?' asked Crabb, replacing the pocket book in his tunic.

'Yes, Anne Cleaves. I found out today that Stapleford had been treating Anne Cleaves, for some unknown medical condition, for the past six months or so. What if Stapleford is now anxious to add her body to his list of medical specimens?'

'We would have to wait until after the funeral and then keep the churchyard under close examination.'

'Yes, but remember that Anne Cleaves is not about to be buried here in Upton, like this Sally Owens and Oliver Thompson, but in Mathon churchyard where, if I recall, the site is overlooked by a number of houses in the village. Any nocturnal activity there would be sure to be observed. No, I think that Stapleford will seek to acquire Anne Cleaves's body before then. You say you saw the coffin being taken into Shortcross and Maudlin's premises?'

'Yes, sir.'

'And that manservant Parsons arrived there shortly afterwards? '

'Yes, sir.'

'Then we will also need to keep the undertakers' premises under close observation. I think that Stapleford will make his move tonight. In a few minutes it will be quite dark. I suggest that we all repair to The White Lion for some refreshment before we take up our positions. It may be a long night, gentlemen, but if our luck holds we might just be able to acquire the solution to this case.'

* * *

'Chosen a good night for it, sir,' said a despondent Crabb, after the clock had just struck eleven, as the two men sheltered from the rain inside a shop doorway in Court Street.

'I am sure that something will happen quite soon. I can see that there is still a light burning in one of the windows of the premises,' replied Ravenscroft, determined to ignore the cold damp discomfort of their vigil.

'Shall I go and check up on Hoskings to make sure he still has the horse and trap at the ready and not gone home instead?'

'No, Tom, you may be required here.'

'I still can't believe that man Stapleford is digging up recently buried bodies,' remarked Crabb, stamping his boots on the ground.

'I know. One would have thought that all that kind of thing had ceased long ago. What's that?' asked Ravenscroft moving back into the darkness and tightly gripping Crabb's arm.

'The doors of the yard are opening. That looks like Reuben Thexton, if I am not mistaken,' said Crabb.

The two detectives watched in silence as another of the Thexton brothers came out of the yard, his hands linked round the harness of a horse that was pulling the same wagon that Ravenscroft had seen earlier that day.

'Anne Cleaves's coffin must be inside that wagon,' whispered Ravenscroft, as the vehicle made its way out of the yard and into the street. Reuben Thexton climbed onto the front of the wagon as the man who had opened the doors, now closed them behind the party and disappeared back into the building.

'Lean back. We must be careful not to be seen,' instructed Ravenscroft, as the horse and wagon driven by the two brothers, made a slow progress past them, before turning the corner and disappearing from view.

'Quickly, Tom, we must join Hoskings and the trap and follow them, although I have a shrewd idea where they are going,' said Ravenscroft, as he and Crabb set off in the other direction.

A few quick steps bought them to where the horse and trap were waiting at the side of the road.

'Where the devil is Hoskings?' shouted out Ravenscroft as he and Crabb mounted the trap. 'Hoskings!' 'Shall we wait for him?' asked Crabb, knowing what his superior's answer would be, as he cracked the whip.

'That man is impossible. Take the next turn right and then turn left; that should bring us back into the main street of the town.'

Crabb did as he was instructed, and a few moments later they found themselves heading out of the town and up the slow incline of the road to Little Malvern.

'Not too close, Tom. We don't want them to see us,' shouted Ravenscroft through the rain as the undertaker's wagon came into view. 'It is just as I suspected, we are heading in the direction of Stapleford's house.'

A few minutes later the wagon suddenly turned off to the left.

'That's far enough, Tom. Go into that space at the side of the road and tie up the horse there.'

'Easy there, boy,' said Crabb patting the horse.

'We will go on foot from here,' continued Ravenscroft, as he and Crabb set off at a brisk pace along the narrow lane. 'I don't want to run the chance that we will disturb the Thextons before they can make their delivery.'

'He must be paying them a large sum of money to acquire the body,' muttered Crabb, pulling his hat further down onto his head in an attempt to protect himself from the rain that was driving into his face.

'There they are, outside Stapleford's premises. We will observe events from behind this bush,' said Ravenscroft removing his spectacles and wiping the lenses on his handkerchief in order to clear the water from them.

'That's Parsons holding the door open,' whispered Crabb. 'And there are the two Thexton brothers struggling to carry the coffin into the house.'

'Why don't we go and arrest the lot of them now?' suggested Crabb.

'No, not yet,' replied Ravenscroft, as the doors of the house closed shut once more. 'We will wait a few minutes and see what transpires.'

A few moments later the doors reopened again, and the two Thexton brothers climbed onto the wagon.

'Shall I go and take them now?' asked an anxious Crabb.

'No, Tom. We can arrest them later. We know where they are. It's Stapleford that I am after.'

The horse and wagon suddenly turned and made a hasty retreat from outside the house, and soon made its way from view down the lane.

'Now we will give Stapleford just five minutes. That should be long enough for him to begin his evil work. I want to catch him in the act. It will give me the greatest satisfaction to see that man sent down,' said Ravenscroft, glancing at his watch.

Crabb pulled himself up to his full height and vigorously shook the rain from his sodden hat.

'Right, Tom, I think that should be long enough. Time we got out of this rain,' said the detective after some minutes had elapsed.

They marched up to the front door and banged heavily on the woodwork, repeating their action after a few moments had elapsed.

'I think I can hear the sound of the bolts being drawn back,' said Ravenscroft.

The door slowly opened a few inches and the wrinkled face of the manservant Parsons could be seen through the narrow gap.

'Yes, Thexton?' asked Parsons mistaking the figure in the darkness for one of the undertakers.

'No, it is not Thexton,' said Ravenscroft pushing open the door and brushing past the startled manservant. 'Where is Stapleford?'

'The master has retired for the evening. I don't understand—' protested Parsons.

'Crabb, let's make for his laboratory at the back of the house,' retorted Ravenscroft leading the way down the corridor.

'Really, sir, I must protest."

'Protest as much as you like, Parsons, but we are the law, and we have strong reasons to suppose that a serious crime has taken place here tonight,' said Ravenscroft, throwing open the door of the room that he knew contained Stapleford's specimen jars.

'He's not here sir,' said Crabb, his eyes sweeping across the room.

'Where is your master?' demanded Ravenscroft.

'I told you sir, that the master has already retired for the night.'

'Then we shall rouse him from his slumbers. Crabb, up those stairs as quickly as you can,' instructed Ravenscroft.

'That will not be necessary, Inspector,' said Stapleford, appearing suddenly in the hallway. 'What is the meaning of the intrusion?'

'We have reason to believe that you are in possession of the body of Miss Anne Cleaves,' said Ravenscroft confronting his adversary.

Stapleford laughed as he turned away. 'Have you gone out of your mind, Ravenscroft? You really are taking things too far. The last time I saw Miss Cleaves was last night when I examined her body at Mathon Manor.'

'We have just witnessed the Thexton brothers' arrival outside your premises,' said Ravenscroft observing that Stapleford had suddenly turned a whiter colour.

'That is indeed so,' stuttered the doctor, after a few moments of awkward silence had elapsed.

'We saw them bring in the coffin,' said Crabb.

'Yes, gentlemen, you are quite correct, but the coffin did not contain the body of Miss Cleaves, I can assure you,' replied Stapleford recovering his composure.

'Then perhaps you would care to tell just what was inside?'

'Certainly; the coffin was of a new design that I had recently drawn up plans for, to be used after my own demise of course. The Thextons were merely delivering the casket to me for my inspection,' said Stapleford, offering a brief smile of satisfaction.

'Nonsense!' retorted Ravenscroft. 'I do not believe such a story for one minute. A coffin delivered late at night under the cover of darkness, which by the way the men were struggling to carry it into your house, was far from empty.'

'The inside of the coffin was lined with lead. I want to make sure that when I die my body will be secure in its final resting place.'

'No doubt safe from body snatchers such as you, Stapleford,' uttered an angry Crabb.

'Really, Ravenscroft, I think you should have better control over your inferiors. This will not look good for both of you in court. Now, I have given you a satisfactory explanation for what has taken place here tonight, so I suggest that you and your constable leave as soon as possible,' Stapleford sneered.

'That is all very well, Stapleford. If this coffin does not contain the body of Miss Cleaves as you say, then you will have no objection if we examine the item,' said Ravenscroft, determined not to be denied, now that he had come this far.

'Well, actually, I do object most strongly. My word should be enough for you. Now please go. Parsons, show these policemen out,' instructed Stapleford.

'Where does that door go to?' asked Ravenscroft, suddenly pointing to a door at side of the corridor.

'It is no concern of yours, but if you must insist, as I suppose that you will, the door is the entrance to a cellar that runs underneath the property.'

'Open the door, or we will break it down,' ordered Ravenscroft.

'My dear Inspector, there is no need for such heroics. As I have said, the door opens out onto a flight of steps that go down under the house. You will find nothing there, I assure you. I have not been down there for years, have I, Parsons?'

'Er . . . no, sir,' stuttered the manservant taken aback by the sudden question.

'Then you will have no objection if we go down there and look for ourselves,' persisted Ravenscroft, trying the handle and finding it locked.

'This is absurd,' countered Stapleford.

'Crabb, lend your shoulder to this door, if you will,' instructed Ravenscroft.

'Yes, sir,' answered Crabb, beginning to take a run at the woodwork.

'All right man! No need for that,' said Stapleford, reluctantly reaching into his jacket pocket and bringing out a large bunch of keys. 'I tell you, this will do you no good at all. It is quite damp and unpleasant down there.'

'Open the door, sir!' demanded Ravenscroft.

Stapleford searched through a number of keys on his ring, until he eventually found one, which he placed in the lock.

'After you, gentlemen,' said Stapleford opening the door.

'After you, sir,' insisted Ravenscroft.

'You can remain here, Parsons,' said Stapleford stepping through the entrance and holding the oil lamp in front of him.

Ravenscroft and Crabb cautiously followed the doctor down the flight of stairs, and soon found themselves standing in a dark, dank, empty room.

'There you are, gentleman. It is as I said, just an empty cellar,' said Stapleford.

Ravenscroft thought he heard the sound of triumph in those words as the doctor held the lamp above his head.

'What is that over there?' asked Ravenscroft, straining to see round the room in the gloomy light.

'Oh, that's just a door. It just leads to a small storeroom, I believe.'

'Give me the lamp,' said Ravenscroft.

'Really, Ravenscroft, I have done all that you ask,' protested Stapleford.

'The lamp, sir!' demanded Ravenscroft firmly.

Stapleford looked at Ravenscroft sternly, before reluctantly handing it over.

Closely followed by Crabb, Ravenscroft opened the door. Holding the lamp high he could see that the walls of this new, inner room were painted white, and that a large table stood in the middle of the room upon which lay a coffin.

The two men quickly moved forward.

'The lid is still undone. Take the other side and lift it up, Crabb,' said Ravenscroft.

The policemen lifted up the wooden lid.

'Oh my God!' exclaimed Crabb recoiling from the contents inside the casket.

'I think we have found Anne Cleaves,' added Ravenscroft, quickly replacing the top of the coffin. 'Now, Dr Stapleford, what have you to say about this?'

Suddenly the door slammed to behind them.

'Stapleford!' cried out Ravenscroft dashing over to the closed door. 'Damn the man. He has locked us in!'

CHAPTER EIGHT

UPTON-UPON-SEVERN

'I am sorry, Tom, I should have known that Stapleford would have done something like this,' said Ravenscroft dispiritedly.

'You were not to know that the man would lock us in here,' replied Crabb attempting to lighten the mood.

'In our eagerness to look inside that box I completely forgot that he was standing behind us.'

'It could be worse, sir. At least he left us the oil lamp, so we are not entirely in the dark.'

'Let us hope the oil lasts out until the morning, or until someone comes to find us.'

'Hoskings knew where we were going,' said Crabb hopefully. 'If he comes up this way he will be sure to find the horse and trap down the lane, and guess that something has happened to us here.'

'I wish I shared your optimism, Tom, but I have a nasty feeling that the lazy fellow gave up waiting for us long ago when we were outside Thextons, and that he went home to his comfortable bed,' replied Ravenscroft gloomily. 'Our wives will be wondering why we have not returned.'

'My Jennie will never believe me when I tell her I spent the night in a cellar with a corpse in a box for company!'

'At least I can confirm your story,' laughed Ravenscroft. 'Let us see what time it is. I see we have been here for nearly two hours now. Time enough for Stapleford to have carried out his escape from the area, I have no doubt.'

'At least we stopped him carrying out his evil work on poor Miss Cleaves.'

'Yes, that is a consolation. When we get out of this we must ensure that she is given a safe and decent burial as soon as possible. This table we are sitting on must be where Stapleford carries out his macabre dissections, before adding the parts of his victims to his anatomical collection. Those must be the tools he uses in the corner over there.'

'The thought sends shivers down my spine,' said Crabb.

'Talking of this table, if we were to move it nearer the wall, there is a small grille at the top. We might be able to stand on it and make ourselves heard if anyone should walk outside,' suggested Ravenscroft.

The two men lifted the coffin from off the table, and placed it in a corner of the room before attempting to move the heavy table.

'Stop, Tom. I don't think we are having much success this way. If we try to drag it across by pulling on this side we might have more success.'

They struggled for some minutes to move the heavy wooden table, gradually heaving it inch by inch nearer to the wall.

'I think that should do. Can you climb up onto the table and reach the grille?' asked Ravenscroft.

Crabb clambered up onto the table, and stretched upwards towards the small narrow aperture at the top of the wall.

'Can you see anything, Tom?'

'I can't quite reach it, sir. All I can see looking upwards is a black sky,' replied Crabb, almost standing on tiptoe.

'Never mind, Tom, come on down. I don't think we can do anything until daylight. All we can do is to listen out for any sounds, then make a loud noise and hope we can be heard.'

Crabb jumped down from the table, the sudden movement occasioned from his descent nearly extinguishing the flame inside the chimney of the oil lamp.

'Sorry, sir.'

'No harm done. Where is that wretched Hoskings? Surely the man could have used his initiative for once and come up here to try and find us. I will see that man dismissed from the police force for incompetence if I have my way,' grumbled Ravenscroft.

'What do you make of this case, sir? Do you think Stapleford killed both Miss Cleaves, and the schoolteacher Smith?' asked Crabb.

'I don't honestly know, Tom. I would certainly like to know why Stapleford visited Anne Cleaves so frequently, but I can't believe that he was her lover.'

'If not, then he couldn't have written all those letters,' added Crabb.

'And if that is the case, he would have had no reason to kill her.'

'He could have killed the schoolmaster with the intention of recovering the corpse at some later date?'

'That could be the case, but if your assumption is correct why would Stapleford try and pass the corpse off as Simon Cleaves? He claimed that he had never met Simon Cleaves, but we know now that he visited his sister a number of times. It does not make sense,' replied Ravenscroft, pacing up and down the room.

'So Stapleford is not our killer?'

'It would appear not, but I am convinced that he is involved in this case somewhere. Why did he lie to us about not knowing the Cleaves family?"

'So, who was Miss Cleaves's lover?'

'Again we have no evidence. Gervase Webster seems the most likely candidate. The two of them are related of course, although not immediate family, I believe: but if that was so why did Simon Cleaves object to the liaison? Then there is Anne Cleaves's recent visit to Glenforest School, where she could have met Smith, but the schoolmaster could not have been her killer because he was dead a week before. She certainly met Horace Smeaton and Marcus Choke on her visit there. I can't see Smeaton being Anne Cleaves's lover, but what about Choke? He appears to have been the last one to have seen Smith alive, and consequently must fall under suspicion. He was quite insistent that his late friend was given a proper burial. Was he acting through compassion, or because of a guilty conscience? I can understand that if Choke was Miss Cleaves's lover why her brother would have objected to such an association. Choke must have meagre means and would have not been considered a worthy suitor for Anne's hand. But then, if Choke is our killer, we must consider why he committed the crimes. What possible reason could there be for Choke to have killed Smith and then Anne Cleaves? No, that does not make any sense either. So we are forced to conclude that Anne Cleaves's lover and murderer is someone who is not known to us at present.'

'We are forgetting one thing sir — those creepy undertakers,' suggested Crabb breaking into Ravenscroft's thoughts.

'You surely don't think that one of those Thexton brothers was Anne Cleaves's lover?'

'No, sir. Highly unlikely, but they are obviously in league with Stapleford.'

'They certainly seem implicated in the abduction of her body. I wonder if Anne Cleaves was the first corpse the Thexton brothers have provided for the doctor? We know that the graves of Sally Owens and Oliver Thompson were disturbed shortly after burial. If Stapleford did dig up the bodies he most probably acted alone, for if the Thextons were in his employ at that date, it would have been easier for them to have supplied Stapleford with the bodies before burial. They could have placed some heavy weights inside the coffins to make it look as though the bodies were still inside.

I wonder who the undertakers were for the burials of Sally Owens and Oliver Thompson. If the families of the deceased used undertakers from Malvern, then that would explain why Stapleford had to resort to retrieving the bodies after burial. We will need to find that out, and we will certainly bring in those men for questioning once we are out of here.'

'This certainly seems a difficult—' began Crabb.

'Hush, Tom! I thought I heard something outside. Quickly, up onto the table. See if you hear anything,' interrupted Ravenscroft suddenly.

Crabb leapt onto the table.

'What can you see or hear, Tom?' asked Ravenscroft eagerly.

'There is nothing, sir. I can't quite reach the opening.'

'Here, Tom, if I get up onto the table and support you on my shoulders that should help,' suggested Ravenscroft.

'Right, sir — that's better. I can see out now. There's a moving light in the distance, like someone carrying a lantern,' strained Crabb, trying to see out into the night sky.

'Give out a shout,' instructed Ravenscroft.

Crabb called out at the top of his voice.

'Nothing, sir, but I think the lantern is getting nearer.'

'Can you hear anything?'

'No, sir. I'll give them another shout. Help! Help!'

'Is there any reply?'

'No. It's Hoskings, sir. Hoskings! Hoskings! Over here! We are over here, you silly man!'

'What is happening?' asked Ravenscroft straining to support Crabb's weight.

'The man must be completely deaf. He's walked away again,' replied Crabb, angrily.

'Here, Tom, if I pass the lamp up to you, run it across the opening, back and forth. He might then see the light. That might stop him in his tracks,' instructed Ravenscroft.

'Hoskings! Hoskings!' cried out Crabb again as he took the lamp and carried out Ravenscroft's instructions. 'We are over here, man! We are here!'

'Constable Crabb?' said the policeman bending down on the ground so that his illuminated faced assumed an almost ghostly appearance in the surrounding darkness, on the other side of the opening.

'We are locked in the cellar, Hoskings. I'm here with Inspector Ravenscroft. Let us out!' shouted Crabb.

'Right, sir, yes sir, right away, sir,' stuttered the confused policeman, before disappearing from view.

'Thank God!' exclaimed a relieved Ravenscroft. 'I don't think we could have spent another hour in this dreadful place.'

After a minute or two elapsed the two policemen were disturbed by the cries of Hoskings through the grille. 'Front door seems to be locked, sir.'

'Then break it down, man!' shouted an annoyed and impatient Ravenscroft, striding up and down the room.

'Get on with it, Hoskings!' added Crabb.

'Where the devil is the man? What is taking him so long?' demanded Ravenscroft.

'Can't find anything to break down the door, sir,' came back the constable's cry after two or three more minutes had elapsed.

'Then break one of the windows and let yourself in that way. Use your initiative, Hoskings. There is a door at the end of the main corridor, on the left-hand side, which leads down to an outer room, which in turn leads into here,' shouted Ravenscroft.

'Right, sir, yes, sir, will do, sir—' shouted back the constable.

'For goodness sake, Hoskings, get on with it quickly, man!'

'Yes, sir,' replied the policeman disappearing from view once more.

'It will be next month before we get out of here, if Hoskings has his way,' grumbled Ravenscroft.

A few moments later the two detectives were rewarded by the sound of a heavy bolt being drawn back and the gradual opening of the door.

'You took your time, Hoskings,' complained Ravenscroft, striding out of the room.

'Sorry, sir,' said the policeman.

'And where the devil were you when we came back to collect the trap?' asked Ravenscroft.

'Sorry, sir. It was all that ale we drank at the Lion. I held out as long as I could—'

'I am not interested in the state of your bladder, Hoskings,' replied Ravenscroft making his way up the stairs, closely followed by his two colleagues. 'I presume that Stapleford has left the house?'

'Yes, sir.'

'Where is the trap?'

'Just at the end of the drive, sir,' answered the forlorn policeman.

'Right, Constable Crabb and I will take that, and return to the station. I want to prepare a report to send to headquarters in the morning, together with a description of Stapleford, so that officers in the Three Counties can be alerted to any possible sightings.'

'What do you want me to do, sir?' asked Hoskings.

'Stay here. The body of Miss Cleaves is inside a coffin in the room we have just left. Secure the bolts and wait until I can send someone over from the undertakers in Ledbury to collect the body,' instructed Ravenscroft.

'But, sir, it is one o'clock in the morning,' protested Hoskings.

'I don't care what time it is, Hoskings. You will remain here until the undertakers arrive. I don't want that body disappearing again. Do you understand that, Constable? Quite frankly, Hoskings, I am not sure that you are suitable for the position to which you have been appointed,' said Ravenscroft raising his voice.

'Yes, sir. Sorry, sir,' replied the subdued constable turning away.

'Right, Tom, back to the station.'

* * *

'Do have another piece of toast, Samuel,' said Lucy at breakfast later that morning.

'I am sorry I disturbed you when I came in last night,' said Ravenscroft, ignoring his wife's offer. 'It must have been nearly three.'

'Three-thirty to be precise.'

'I'm sorry. I had to complete that report and description and then wake up the undertakers in Ledbury to tell them to collect Anne Cleaves's body. They were not too pleased either to be woken from their slumbers,' apologized Ravenscroft, pouring himself out another cup of tea.

'It must have been quite awful for you to be locked in that cellar with only a dead body for company,' sympathized Lucy.

'It was fortunate that Tom was with me, and that Constable Hoskings eventually came to rescue us, or we would still have been there now.'

'I hope someone will apprehend that terrible man. I can imagine nothing more ghastly that cutting up dead people, and then keeping parts of them in glass jars.'

'It is almost back to the days of Burke and Hare. I thought that finished a long time ago.'

'And those terrible undertakers, they must have been in league with your Dr Stapleford. How can they have done such a thing?'

'Oh, money, I expect. It always comes down to money.'

'Well, I think it is a despicable thing. In your hour of need and distress, you should at least be able to trust those you have instructed to take care of your loved ones.'

'Indeed. Now, my dear, you must excuse me if I hurry away,' said Ravenscroft, rising from his seat and nearly knocking over the tea cup in the process.

'So what will you do today?' asked Lucy.

'Go and see what those undertakers have to say for themselves. Then we will return to Mathon. I hope that Gervase Webster will have arrived, and that he can provide us with the answers we so desperately need regarding this case.'

'Take care,' called out Lucy, as her husband made his way out of the room.

'I am sorry, my dear,' said Ravenscroft, quickly returning and kissing his wife on the cheek. 'I cannot tell you what time I will return.'

'I know, Samuel,' sighed Lucy.

'And we must have words about Richard's education.'

'Yes, but go, Samuel. Go. Go now.'

* * *

'Who the devil is that banging on the door of the station?' asked Ravenscroft as he and Crabb approached the outside of the small building.

'I think it is those wretched Thextons,' answered Crabb pulling on the reins and drawing the trap to a halt.

'Thank goodness you are here, Inspector,' said an agitated Reuben Thexton coming forwards to meet the detectives.

'Something terrible has happened!' exclaimed an equally disturbed Benjamin Thexton.

'Most terrible!' added Simeon Thexton.

'Pray, gentlemen, what has occurred?' asked Ravenscroft.

'Miss Cleaves's coffin has been taken!' announced Reuben.

'Removed from our premises in the dead of night, was it not, Brothers?' said Benjamin firmly.

'It was indeed, Brothers,' confirmed Simeon.

'The good lady was resting in our sanctuary when we locked up for the evening,' continued Reuben.

'And gone when we arrived this morning,' said Benjamin, shaking his head in a forlorn manner.

'A most terrible occurrence, Brothers,' remarked Simeon raising his eyes upwards to the sky.

'I think you had better come inside, gentlemen,' answered an intrigued Ravenscroft, attempting to open the door. 'Do we have a key, Constable Crabb?'

' I believe Constable Hoskings has the only key.'

'Strange. I thought we left the building open when we left last night.'

'Then Hoskings must have locked it again?' suggested Crabb.

'He could be inside; bang on the door again, Constable,' instructed Ravenscroft.

After some moments, the sound of a lock being turned on the inside of the door could be heard.

'Hoskings!' called out Ravenscroft. 'Let us in, man!'

The door opened quickly to reveal the bleary-eyed and untidy constable.

'Out of our way, Hoskings,' said an annoyed Ravenscroft, pushing past the unfortunate policeman. 'Gentlemen, if you will follow me.'

The three undertakers filed into the office.

'Now perhaps one of you could tell me what has happened?' asked Ravenscroft throwing his hat down onto the counter.

The three brothers looked at one another in silence, each not wanting to speak before the others.

'Well? Mr Reuben, if you will.'

'As we said Inspector, when we left our premises last night, Miss Cleaves's coffin was resting in the inner room, and when we arrived here this morning we found that the lock of the building had been forced, and that the coffin had been removed. It is all quite distressing. Nothing like this has happened to us before,' said Reuben.

'Quite distressing, Brothers,' interjected Benjamin.

'And what time did you leave the building yesterday evening?' asked Ravenscroft before the other brother could add his contribution to the conversation.

'Just after ten I believe,' answered Reuben.

'And what time did you arrive this morning?'

'Well, just a few minutes ago. We came here straight away to report the matter,' said Benjamin.

'Where can poor Miss Cleaves be?' asked a worried Reuben.

'Who can have been so heartless as to have carried out this terrible deed?' said a mournful Benjamin.

'Well, gentlemen, this is all very interesting, but I have to tell you that it is all nonsense,' said Ravenscroft firmly. 'What would you say if I told you that Constable Crabb and myself witnessed you removing Miss Cleaves's coffin from your premises, just after eleven o'clock yesterday evening, and that we followed you out of the town, to where you delivered your load to Dr Stapleford?'

The three brothers again looked at one another, mystified expressions on their faces.

'Well, what have you got to say to that?' asked Ravenscroft impatiently.

'I think you must be mistaken, Inspector,' replied Reuben after a long pause. 'After we left our premises yesterday evening, my brothers and I retired to the Plough, by the river, to partake of some liquid refreshment. We were there until after midnight.'

'So you see, Inspector, you are very much mistaken,' said Simeon adopting a reproachful manner.

'May we suggest that you commence a search for Miss Cleaves's coffin, as soon as possible?' suggested Reuben.

'With the utmost degree of urgency,' nodded Benjamin again.

'Her relatives will be sorely distressed, will they not, Brothers?' added Simeon.

'Stop all this nonsense!' cried out an annoyed Ravenscroft. 'You know perfectly what has happened to Miss Cleaves. You were seen taking the coffin to Dr Stapleford's residence and unloading it there. Furthermore the body has now been removed for safekeeping, to a firm of undertakers in Ledbury.'

'I see,' said Reuben a sorrowful expression on his face.

'We cannot understand this, Inspector. You say that you saw my brothers and I carrying out this terrible deed.' said Reuben.

'I do indeed. Constable Crabb can bear witness to the fact,' replied Ravenscroft.

'Indeed sir,' confirmed the policeman.

'But we were in the Plough at the time you state, Inspector. There are at least a dozen people there who can confirm our presence,' said Benjamin in a matter-of-fact tone of voice.

'The inspector is clearly mistaken, Brother,' added Simeon. 'It was a very dark and somewhat inclement night. Quite clearly you mistook these vile intruders for my brothers and me.'

'Were you responsible for carrying out the burial arrangements for Sally Owens?' asked Ravenscroft, realizing that he was making little headway with his questioning, and deciding to change the subject.

'Sally Owens? That was the young lady who passed away quite suddenly last year, was it not, Brothers?' enquired Reuben.

'I believe so,' answered Benjamin.

'But no, Inspector, we did not carry out the young lady's funeral. I believe Oldcastle and Plunkett of Malvern may have carried out the preparation and burial,' said Simeon.

'And Oliver Thompson, did you carry out his funeral arrangements?' continued Ravenscroft.

'I believe not, Brothers?' asked Reuben of his two siblings.

'Gaskett and Son of Malvern Link,' smiled Simeon.

'How long have you known Dr Stapleford?' sighed Ravenscroft, feeling that he was becoming more and more frustrated by the supercilious manner of the three undertakers.

'We know of the said gentleman of course, but we are not intimate in anyway with the good doctor,' answered Simeon.

'We never meet socially,' said Benjamin.

'Only in a professional capacity, is it not, Brothers?' asked Reuben.

'How many of the doctor's former patients have you buried?' asked Ravenscroft, finding the answers more and more confusing.

'I would estimate five or six, would that be correct?' asked Simeon.

'A trifle over-estimated,' disagreed Reuben. 'Only three I believe.'

'I am sure it was more likely to have been six,' corrected Simeon.

'We would have to consult our records,' smiled Benjamin.

'I would like a list of all those people, by this afternoon,' demanded Ravenscroft.

'Of course, Inspector,' smiled Benjamin again. 'We will do anything to assist the police with their inquiries.'

'Now, I think it is time we attended to our duties,' remarked Reuben beginning to move towards the entrance of the room.

'Indeed so, Brother Reuben,' said Benjamin in support of his brother.

'We wish you good day, Inspector,' added Simeon.

'How much did Stapleford pay you for the body?' called out Ravenscroft as the brothers left the room, but if he expected an answer there was none forthcoming.

'Shall I go after them and arrest them?' asked Crabb.

'It will be no use. We are dealing with very cunning men. They must have known that we visited Stapleford's house and recovered the coffin, so they thought they would approach us first with their cock and bull story before we could march round there and arrest them. I have no doubt that if we went to the Plough there would be at least a dozen of their friends, who would happily commit perjury by claiming that they were drinking ale there at the same time that we saw them delivering and unloading the body! If we bought a prosecution against them I am sure it would collapse at the first hurdle in any court in the land. It would be our word against the three of theirs, and their dozen witnesses. No, our undertakers have outsmarted us for the present,' sighed Ravenscroft.

'The sanctimonious scoundrels,' muttered Crabb.

'Those brothers are well suited to their trade; all forced piety and faked concern, when their main desire in life is to acquire as much money as they can by assisting that man Stapleford. We should have arrested them last night when we caught them in the act, but I am sure that if we bide our time another opportunity will soon present itself.'

'Do you think they could be hiding Stapleford?'

'There is that possibility of course, but I think it is more than likely that the doctor has left the area.'

'I should like to go back to his house and smash all those bottles and jars,' said Crabb enthusiastically.

'I don't think that would be a good idea. I would have to arrest you for wilful damage, and that would never do. Far better I approach Bart's and see if they would like to add some of the specimens to their collection. We may as well provide some assistance to the extension of medical knowledge, if we can.'

'Would you like me and Hoskings to keep the undertakers' premises under observation, in case Stapleford shows up, or they start moving bodies around?' asked Crabb.

'No, I don't think that the Thextons will attempt anything so rash at the moment, when they know that we regard them as our main suspects. I think we will do better by returning to Mathon Manor and questioning Gervase Webster. Where is Hoskings?' asked Ravenscroft picking up his hat from off the counter.

'I think he went in the other room, sir.'

'No, he does not appear to be in here.'

'I'll check in the cells,' offered Crabb, disappearing from view.

Ravenscroft made his way down the damp, forbidding corridor.

'Look here, sir,' said Crabb standing at the entrance to one of the cells.

Ravenscroft looked into the small enclosure and discovered the stout policeman lying asleep in one corner of the cell, his heavy breathing interspersed with the sound of the occasional snore.

'The lazy good-for-nothing!' exclaimed Crabb. 'Shall I wake him?'

'No, leave the poor man in peace. If fortune shines on us perhaps someone will make their way in here and lock him in for the rest of the week,' replied Ravenscroft turning on his heel.

* * *

As the trap made its way down the long avenue of trees at Mathon Manor, a lone figure could be glimpsed walking across the lawns.

'Who is that?' asked Crabb.

'A young gentleman who goes by the name of Timothy Muncaster,' replied Ravenscroft.

'Who is Timothy Muncaster, sir?'

'A newly qualified barrister I encountered on my visit to the Temple in London. He is a most amusing and agreeable fellow. Gervase Webster sent him down here yesterday, as he was unable to come himself.'

'I see.'

'Mr Muncaster!' called out Ravenscroft as the trap drew nearer.

'Good morning, Inspector,' replied the young lawyer, smiling as he removed his hat.

'I trust I find you well?' asked Ravenscroft.

'Middling, my dear sir, middling,' replied Muncaster adopting a melancholic air. 'I just had to get away from that dreadful dingy house. Much as I dislike the countryside, the air out here is preferable to the stuffy solemnity to be found inside that building. I find death somewhat unsettling. Never quite know what to say in such circumstances.'

Ravenscroft smiled. 'Has Mr Webster arrived yet?'

'He sent me a telegram, which arrived early this morning, telling me to collect him from Colwall Station at midday. He is not in a good mood, I can tell you.'

'Then perhaps you can return to London quite soon, now that you have fulfilled your duty here?' suggested Ravenscroft.

'Gervase says I can leave on the three-thirty this afternoon. Must say I can't wait. If all goes well I should be back in the metropolis by nightfall. A rather large juicy piece of mutton has my name on it at The Cheshire Cheese in Fleet Street,' brightened up Muncaster. 'Meanwhile I have drafted a reply to your letter from Rawlinson, for your consideration.'

'Ah well, circumstances have somewhat altered since we spoke yesterday. Doctor Stapleford has taken flight,' said Ravenscroft.

'Tell me more?' asked the young lawyer eagerly.

'We caught Dr Stapleford taking possession of Miss Cleaves's body from the undertakers' in Upton. It seems that he was anxious to acquire it to aid his medical research.'

'I say, what exciting stuff!'

'However, before we could arrest him he managed to escape. We have posted notices for his arrest, and when he is apprehended, as I trust he soon will be, he will not be in any position to bring any charges against me. So, I am afraid I have rather wasted your time.'

'No matter, my dear sir; think no more of it.'

'You must let me know if I am in your debt.'

'No debt to be paid, sir, but should you find yourself up in London anytime, you may have the honour of buying me a glass or two of the best Madeira.'

'That will be my privilege, Mr Muncaster, but I shall insist on a bottle rather than a glass,' smiled Ravenscroft, as he and Crabb set off down the rest of the drive.

As they arrived at the front entrance, Mansfield came out to meet them.

'Good morning to you, Mansfield. I understand that Mr Webster has arrived.'

'He has indeed, sir. If you would care to follow me to the drawing room, I will see if he is free to speak to you.'

Ravenscroft and Crabb made their way up the steps, into the main hall and continued on to the room at the front of the building.

'Ah, Ravenscroft, this is a bad business indeed,' said Webster rising as they entered the room.

'I am sorry for your loss, sir,' said Ravenscroft sympathetically. 'How is Lady Cleaves bearing up?'

'Not well, I am afraid. She remains in her room, and cannot see anyone. All this has come as rather a shock to her, as I am sure you appreciate,' said the lawyer with a serious air as he indicated with his hand that Ravenscroft should take one of the seats.

'Of course; this must be a difficult time for your family.'

'Who can have committed such an atrocity? To break into one's house and then to murder an innocent young lady of Anne's standing and reputation is a diabolical affront. I trust you are doing all that you can to find this evil perpetrator?'

'We are following many lines of inquiry at present.'

'If you need more officers I can write to your superior requesting additional assistance,' suggested Webster.

'That will not be necessary at this stage of the investigation. I have to tell you that since yesterday, there have been developments in the case,' said Ravenscroft, uncomfortable at the news that he was about to impart.

'Please proceed with your news, Inspector, if you will,' said Webster looking intently at the detective.

'Yesterday your cousin's body was taken to Shortcross and Maudlin's funeral parlour in Upton-upon-Severn. At eleven o'clock in the evening, Constable Crabb and I witnessed the undertakers delivering the coffin to Dr Stapleford.'

'Stapleford? Whatever would he want with Anne's body?'

'It seems that the doctor is rather fond of carrying out dissections on recently deceased bodies, in order to further his anatomical research.'

'Good God!'

'Fortunately we were able to prevent such a violation taking place.'

'Thank goodness for that,' said a relieved Webster. 'And where is my cousin's body now?'

'The coffin has been removed to a firm of reputable undertakers in Ledbury. She will be quite safe there, I can assure you. My constable will provide Mr Mansfield with all the details.'

'I see.'

'Can you think of anyone who might have wanted to harm your cousin?' asked Ravenscroft.

'Good heavens no! She was a dear, sweet girl, without an enemy in the world.'

'We believe that Miss Cleaves was in a relationship prior to her death.'

'Relationship? What kind of relationship?' asked Webster.

'She had been corresponding with a gentleman who is at present unknown to us. We believe that on the afternoon of her death, she had arranged to meet this man in her bedroom. It was this man who murdered your cousin, Mr Webster, and who then removed the incriminating letters before effecting his escape,' said Ravenscroft in a matter-of-fact tone of voice, as he studied Webster's face closely for any reaction to his disclosure.

'Forgive me, Inspector, but how do you know all this?'

'Miss Cleaves's maid has confirmed to us that her mistress had received a number of these letters in recent weeks, and we also found evidence which indicates that your cousin left a window open in a room, so that her lover could make his way unobserved into the house.'

'But why; why did Anne agree to meet this man in her own bedroom, of all places?' asked a concerned Webster. 'Would it not have been more prudent to have met elsewhere?'

'Indeed so, but the man's main motive seems to have been the recovery of the letters. It seems that your cousin must have been on quite intimate terms with this man to have facilitated his access her bedroom.'

'I find all this quite extraordinary,' uttered the lawyer.

'You have no idea who this man could have been?'

'No. Anne certainly never said anything to me about this matter.'

'We know that her brother did not approve of this association. He was heard, by one of the servants, to complain about her receiving such letters. This would suggest that the man might have been of an inferior station to the family. There is no one at all that you might think could be this man?' asked Ravenscroft.

'No. As I have said, there is no one at all.'

'We also understand that Miss Cleaves had received a number of visits from Dr Stapleford in recent weeks. I wonder if your cousin ever confided in you regarding the state of her health?'

'No. She mentioned nothing to me, although I must admit that upon the last two or three occasions that we met, I did consider that she looked rather paler than usual. In fact, the more I think about it, she did seem a trifle out of sorts.'

'Could you elaborate further, sir?' asked Ravenscroft, curious to know more.

'Well, I can't really tell you much, other than the fact that she seemed to be somewhat lacking in her usual outward demeanour, if you know what I mean. The disappearance of her brother must also have caused her some concern.'

'But she said nothing to you regarding this matter?'

'No. Look, Inspector, I don't know where all this is getting us. My cousin has been brutally murdered. I think you would be better employed carrying out a search in the immediate neighbourhood to see if anyone remembers this man entering or leaving the house yesterday afternoon,' said Webster, agitatedly as he rose quickly from his seat.

'We have already made extensive enquiries in the area, but I would like to take this opportunity of questioning the servants further. In my experience it is always the servants who are aware of any dark secrets that may be hidden in such establishments as this,' said Ravenscroft.

'You must do as you will, Ravenscroft, but I tell you I want this evil man caught as soon as possible, and unless you can solve this crime by tomorrow morning, I will take further measures to ensure that some men from the Yard are sent down here to take over the case. I trust I make myself clear on this point?'

'I understand you perfectly, sir. Now, if you will excuse us.'

* * *

The two policemen made their way into the kitchen where they found the maid, Charlotte, sitting at the table talking to a stout elderly woman, whom Ravenscroft recognized as the cook. Both women rose as the detectives entered the room.

'Please do not rise on my account,' said Ravenscroft indicating that the women should remain seated. 'I rather hoped that I would find you here, Charlotte. I would like to ask you a few more questions about your mistress, if you don't mind?'

'Would you like me to go, sir?' asked the cook.

'No. You might be able to help us with our enquiries as well, Mrs Wills,' smiled Ravenscroft seating himself at the table.

'Perhaps you would like a glass of our homemade elderflower cordial?' offered the cook.

'That would be very acceptable,' said Ravenscroft.

'Your constable looks as though he could do with some refreshment.'

'Indeed so, ma'am,' said Crabb seating himself eagerly in one of the other chairs.

The cook poured out two glasses and handed them over.

'This is uncommonly good,' said Crabb, after he had downed almost all of the glass.

'Then you shall have more,' smiled the cook.

'Charlotte, we understand that your mistress received a number of visits from Dr Stapleford in the weeks before her death. Do you know what ailed your mistress?'

'I don't really know, sir. She always saw him alone. She never told me why the doctor visited her,' replied Charlotte.

'Had you noticed any change in Miss Cleaves's condition during those weeks?' continued Ravenscroft.

'Not really. She wasn't ill, as far as I could see, but she seemed quite concerned about something.'

'Can you enlighten us further?'

'She never spoke of anything, but to me she seemed as though she had something on her mind.'

'That was before her brother left the house, or after?'

'It was before, sir.'

'Where did these consultations with Dr Stapleford usually take place?'

'She usually saw him in the drawing room, sir, although once or twice she and the doctor did meet in her bedroom.'

'And you were not present at these meetings, I think you said?'

'I was not, sir.'

'You did not consider that this was somewhat indiscreet behaviour on the part of your mistress?' suggested Ravenscroft.

'Yes, sir, but then he was a doctor, wasn't he?' replied the maid.

'He was indeed,' smiled Ravenscroft. 'Do you recall whether Dr Stapleford prescribed any medication for your mistress?'

'Yes, sir, I believe he did.'

'Can you recall what this medicine might have been?'

'No, sir,' replied the maid, somewhat downcast.

'That is a pity,' Ravenscroft sighed.

'There was an empty bottle on her dressing table I saw once.'

'Do you recall what was written on the label?' asked Ravenscroft, hopefully.

'Yes, sir. I think it was Fowler's Solution,' she answered.

'Interesting; the standard cure for all ills,' said Ravenscroft.

'I also saw a bottle of Valentine's Beef Juice once,' added the maid.

'A not uncommon remedy taken to improve one's constitution I believe. Was your mistress ever sick or ill in any way after taking these medicines?'

'No, I don't think so, sir.'

'Thank you, Charlotte, you have been most informative,' said Ravenscroft, rising from the table.'

'You will catch this dreadful fiend?' asked a tearful Mrs Wills.

'I sincerely hope so,' replied Ravenscroft taking his leave. 'Good day to you, ladies.'

* * *

'This is a devil of a case,' said Ravenscroft, feeling frustrated by events, as he and Crabb walked across the lawns. 'Schoolmaster in all probability murdered; local landowner gone missing; mistress of the house cruelly murdered; unknown woman in Ludlow not found; love letters stolen; family doctor attempts to gain possession of the corpse — none of it seems to make any sense, and yet everything must be related to this same case in one way or another; it is just that we cannot see the connections. What is all this about, Tom? I just wish I knew.'

'I wish I could contribute something enlightening,' said Crabb sympathetically.

'I had hoped that Webster would provide some answers to this mystery, but he seems as much in the dark as we are.'

'Still cannot say that I like the man. There is something about him. I don't feel that he can be trusted. I never did like lawyers; too smart for their own good.'

'You could be right. There might be something he is not telling us, but I feel I cannot press him further at this time. The death of his cousin must have come as a shock,' replied Ravenscroft, pausing on his walk to look back at the large house. 'I wonder what dark secrets lie hidden between the walls of that rather austere building.'

'What do you think Stapleford was treating Anne Cleaves for?' asked Crabb.

'I was hoping that the servants would have known the answer to that question, but all we know are the names of two bottles that were in her possession. Fowler's Solution is taken by many people for a range of things — to improve circulation, for weight gain, to counteract depression, cure stomach problems, amongst other things. It seems to be a universal cure for practically anything and everything. I do know that it must be taken in small, diluted quantities due to the arsenic it contains.'

'Valentine's Beef Juice is pretty harmless. Mrs Crabb swears by it, particularly in the winter months.'

'I believe so. The mixture is thought to be very nutritious.'

'Do you think that Stapleford was trying to kill Miss Cleaves by increasing the dose of the Fowler's?'

'You mean so that he could hasten her death in order to obtain her corpse for dissection? Anne Cleaves was certainly looking pale and drawn whenever we interviewed her, but I wouldn't say that she was unusually thin, and the servants do not recall her being either sick or ill, which she might have been had the arsenic been of a sufficient quantity, so I think we must rule out that line of inquiry. Nevertheless it might have been valuable if we had learned what in fact Stapleford was treating her for.'

'You still believe that Stapleford was not Anne Cleaves's lover?'

'We know that Stapleford visited the house a number of times during the past few weeks, and that the two of them were alone during his consultations, but I still cannot see him as her lover. I would like to get my hands on that evil man though so that we could arrive at the truth. Now that we have alerted all the surrounding police forces to keep a look out for him I would hope for an early arrest.'

'What do you think has happened to Simon Cleaves?' asked Crabb as the pair resumed their walk.

'I only wish I knew. It was his supposed death which started all this off.'

'He must be dead, sir.'

'Yes, but if that is the case, where is his body?'

'Buried somewhere, burnt to ashes, or lying at the bottom of the Severn,' suggested Crabb.

'Yes, that could be so, but if that is the case, why was he killed?'

'Out of revenge, killed as the result of some argument, gone abroad and fallen overboard during the passage — any of these could be a possible reason,' answered Crabb.

'If he is dead, then it is highly possible that he was killed by the same person who murdered his sister,' continued Ravenscroft thinking out loud. 'We know that Simon Cleaves did not approve of his sister's association with the man, so that might explain why he was killed, but if that was so, why would the murderer then go on to kill the sister? Unless of course, she knew that her lover had killed her brother and threatened to reveal his identity?'

'If Stapleford killed Simon Cleaves he might have already dissected his body, in which case parts of him could be in some of those glass jars,' interrupted Crabb.

'Now that would be too macabre to contemplate, Tom. However, all this is pure conjecture at the present time. We cannot say that Simon Cleaves is indeed dead until we have recovered his body. Let's go over to the stables there and have another word with the stable lad. I want to learn more about Simon Cleaves. There just might be a chance that the lad knows something.'

The two men quickened their pace across the lawns until they reached a range of rambling farm buildings situated near to one side of the main house.

Ravenscroft crossed over the cobbled courtyard and pushed open one of the stable doors.

'Good day to you, sir,' said a young sandy-haired youth, holding a brush and comb, who was standing beside a dapple grey horse.

'Good day to you. It is William, if I am not mistaken?' asked Ravenscroft.

'It is, sir,' replied the youth.

'Please continue with your work. We would just like to ask you a few questions concerning your master,' said Ravenscroft.

'You've found Master Simon?' asked the stable lad eagerly.

'Unfortunately we have not. I wish I could inform you otherwise. How often did your employer go riding?'

'Two or three times a week, sometimes as many as four.'

'And did Miss Anne like riding as well?'

'Yes, sir, although she only went out once or twice a week,' answered William, busily engaged in brushing down the horse.

'Can you remember what happened on the morning when your master was last seen?'

'Yes, sir. Miss Anne, she came to the stables and collected old Yorke, that's the horse over there, and said she was going out riding. Then not two minutes later Master Simon he came and took old Dibbin.'

'Just a moment,' interrupted Ravenscroft. 'Did you say that it was Miss Anne who went riding first?'

'Yes, sir.'

'Now that is interesting. Miss Cleaves told us that she said farewell to her brother when he left the house that morning.'

'The young lady must have been lying to us,' said Crabb.

'It would seem so. Now, William, are you absolutely sure that it was Miss Anne who left the stables first?'

'Yes.'

'Then you say Mr Cleaves came out quite soon afterwards? Do you recall if he was carrying a bag of any kind, an overnight bag perhaps?' asked Ravenscroft, anxious to know more.

'I don't think so, sir.'

'Did Miss Cleaves say anything to you when she collected the horse?'

'Not much, only that she would probably be an hour or so, that was all I think,' answered William pausing from his labours.

'How was Mr Simon when he came over to the stables?'

'I don't understand you, sir.'

'Well, was your master happy, sad, angry or upset in any way?'

'Yes, sir, I believe he was quite angry.'

'And did Mr Cleaves say anything to you?'

'Yes, sir.'

'And what was that?'

'He said something like — "Now I'll have them. I'll teach him a lesson he won't forget!" '

'"Now I'll have them. I'll teach him a lesson he won't forget",' repeated Ravenscroft. 'You are sure those were the exact words?'

'Yes, sir.'

'Did he say anything else?'

'No, sir.'

'Did either Miss Cleaves, or her brother, say where they were going?'

'No, sir.'

'That is a shame,' said Ravenscroft, shaking his head.

'But I think I know where they might have been going,' said the boy eagerly.

'Where?'

'Miss Cleaves she went that away,' gestured the youth, walking over to the stable door and pointing out to the left. 'She usually went to the old Folly.'

'The old Folly . . . where is that?' asked Crabb.

'It is about two or three miles from here. You goes up there, over that hill, and along the ridge, then across the fields and up again.'

'And you believe that was the way your mistress went that day?' asked Ravenscroft.

'Yes, sir.'

'Then your master came out, saddled the horse — and did he go the same way?'

'Yes. I remember he watched until mistress disappeared from view over the hill, then he galloped after her.'

'Why on earth did you not tell us all about this earlier?' asked Ravenscroft.

'No one asked me,' replied the stable lad somewhat sheepishly.

'No. I suppose no one did,' said Ravenscroft forcing a brief smile. 'William, we would be obliged if you would take us out to see this place.'

'To the old Folly sir?'

'If you would be so kind, it would be much appreciated. My constable and I will follow in our trap.'

* * *

Ravenscroft and Crabb sat in the trap as its wheels bumped over the uneven surface of the ground, William and the horse a few yards ahead of them.

'She lied to us all along, Tom. Anne Cleaves did not watch her brother ride away from the house that morning. She rode out first, with the intention of meeting her lover at this old Folly,' said Ravenscroft, as the trap ran along the top of a ridge.

'That was why Simon Cleaves followed her.'

'Exactly, he wanted to confront Anne and her lover together. "I'll teach him a lesson he won't forget" were his exact words. I fear the worst, Tom, I fear the worst.'

Their journey eventually took them down from the ridge and across some open fields on the other side of the hill, until another track took them slowly up once again.

'That must be the old Folly,' said Crabb pointing to an old tower on top of the hill in the distance.

Ravenscroft said nothing as the trap completed its journey and they saw that William had alighted from his horse in front of the ruined tower.

'This is it, sir,' said the stable lad, as the two detectives stepped out of their trap.

'Not quite so old as it looks,' said Ravenscroft, looking upwards at the old stones that formed the circular building.

'Built by Sir Anthony Cleaves I believe, Master Simon's grandfather, about fifty years ago,' said William.

'You are most informative,' said Ravenscroft. 'I did not know that people still built these follies. Shall we look inside, Crabb?'

'Is it safe?' enquired the constable.

'Yes, sir. I don't think there are any loose stones,' replied William.

Ravenscroft stepped through the opening of the building and found a set of stairs facing him inside the small earthen-floored room. 'I presume these steps will take us to the top?'

'Yes, sir.'

Ravenscroft led the way up along the damp, narrow, winding stairs and after a minute or two had elapsed arrived at the top of the tower.

'Well, Tom, there is certainly a fine view from here,' said Ravenscroft, walking across the wooden floor and looking out at the surrounding countryside. 'I see why Sir Anthony built his folly here. You can certainly see for miles; over there are the Malverns, so close in appearance that one feels you could almost reach out and touch them, while behind us must be the view across the fields towards the Teme Valley, and distant Clee beyond.'

'Must be a hundred feet or more,' said Crabb, peering over the edge, and looking down at the horse and stable lad beneath them.

'So this was where Anne Cleaves went to meet her lover that morning, and where Simon Cleaves must have confronted the couple. I wonder what took place here?' Ravenscroft mused.

'Perhaps we will never know, now that Miss Anne is dead, and her brother still missing,' answered Crabb.

'I cannot see that any sign of a struggle took place here. There are no blood stains on the floor, and no stones seem to have been displaced from the top of the walls. I don't think we can gain anything else by remaining up here.'

They retraced their steps down the circular stairway of the tower, until they reached the ground floor of the building once more.

'I can see nothing in this room either,' said Ravenscroft, stepping out into the daylight.

'Fine view, sir,' smiled the youth.

'Indeed. Tom, let us take a walk around the grounds.'

'What are we looking for?' asked Crabb.

'Anything that might have been dropped, any earth that might have been disturbed, any sign of a struggle that may have taken place,' replied Ravenscroft.

The two detectives began walking around the base of the tower, before widening their circle of exploration.

'What is down there at the bottom of the field? I thought I saw water from the top of the tower,' said Ravenscroft, returning to address the stable lad after a few minutes had elapsed.

'That's just an old pond, sir, down in the hollow,' replied William.

Ravenscroft walked quickly down the slope toward the water, closely followed by Crabb and the stable lad.

'I would not be surprised if some monks lived out here many centuries ago. Ponds such as this were used for breeding and keeping fish, although it has been sadly neglected over the years, hence its rather murky appearance.'

'Looks more like a lake than a pond to me,' said Crabb.

'Stop, Tom! What is this?' said Ravenscroft, suddenly coming to a halt and bending down to retrieve an item from the ground.

'It looks like an old glove to me,' said Crabb.

'That's Master's glove!' exclaimed William.

'Are you sure?' asked Ravenscroft.

'Yes. It is the master's riding glove. I would know it anywhere. He wore it the day he left.'

Ravenscroft looked at Crabb before the two of them quickened their pace.

'This is the pond. Seems quite deep, although one cannot be quite sure how deep it is, due to all the green slime and leaves on the top of the water,' said Ravenscroft.

'What are you thinking, sir?' asked an apprehensive Crabb.

'William, I want you to return to the house as quickly as you can. Then bring out the wagon, and as many men as you can find, and some long poles and other long implements and nets,' instructed Ravenscroft. 'Do you have a canoe or a rowing boat of any kind? If so, bring that back as well.'

'Yes, sir, there is a small rowing boat in the stables. You don't think that the master—?' began the startled youth.

'Just do as I say,' emphasized Ravenscroft raising his voice.

The two watched as the stable lad rode off into the distance.

'If I am not mistaken, Tom, I believe we might just find the answer to all our questions lying down there in this pond!'

CHAPTER NINE

MATHON MANOR

As the afternoon progressed six men stood in silence at the sides of the pond as events unfolded before them — the middle-aged detective with thinning hair and spectacles, conscious that all eyes were upon him, full of feelings of doubt and insecurity that the search he had personally instigated would yield nothing; the young fresh faced constable shuffling his feet, trusting that his superior's judgement would be vindicated, while giving occasional instructions to the men in the boat; the London lawyer striding up and down impatiently, taking out his watch every few minutes and wondering whether the enterprise would prove a waste of time; the youthful barrister straining to observe every aspect of the scene, wishing not to miss anything of importance and realizing that he would not now be returning to the capital that day; the butler standing tall and erect, praying that the search would prove futile, but bracing himself to provide the support he knew the family and servants would need if the day turned bad; the young stable lad not daring to look at the scene before him, racked by feelings of guilt that he had not spoken out sooner and wishing himself anywhere but there at that scene.

'I think this has gone on long enough, Ravenscroft,' said Gervase Webster, breaking the silence. 'The men must have searched practically all of the pond by now. This is obviously a foolish notion of yours.'

'I would like the search to continue for a while longer, Mr Webster. Crabb, tell the men to come nearer to the edge over there,' instructed Ravenscroft.

'Yes, sir,' replied Crabb, waving his arms in the direction of the boat and then shouting out to the men.

'This is quite futile, Ravenscroft,' continued Webster. 'What evidence do you have that suggests that my cousin lies at the bottom of that pond?'

'We know that Mr Cleaves followed Miss Cleaves out here on that fateful morning, and that he must have confronted his sister and her lover. I have no doubt that a fight ensued. We also have the evidence of the glove; in my experience a rider does not just discard his expensive leather glove on the ground and not seek to retrieve it,' answered Ravenscroft, feeling increasingly uneasy, and knowing that he would not be able to prolong the search beyond nightfall.

'I am sorry for all this, Muncaster. It seems that you have missed your train back to London,' said Webster, turning to face the young barrister.

'That is quite all right, Gervase. I would not have missed all this activity for the world. It is not every day that one gets invited to the country and things like this happen — not of course that I would want them to find your cousin at the bottom of that murky old pond, no, not at all,' replied Muncaster embarrassed, realizing that he had perhaps said too much as he turned away and looked down at the ground.

'Over here, sir!' suddenly called out one of the men from the boat gesturing wildly.

Ravenscroft and Crabb ran round to the other side of the pond, closely followed by the rest of the group.

'I think we have got something, sir,' said the second man in the boat.

'Can you bring it to the side,' shouted Ravenscroft in reply.

As the boat neared the edge of the pond, Ravenscroft strained to see what the men were clutching at the back of the boat.

'Oh my God, it must be Simon!' said Webster.

Ravenscroft and Crabb reached out across the water and, grabbing hold of the bundle, pulled it, inch by inch, up onto the bank.

'Heavens, what has happened to his face?' asked Muncaster inquisitively leaning forward to obtain a better view.

'How can we be sure it is Simon. . .?' asked an ashen-faced Webster, his voice trailing away.

The group turned round suddenly as the stable lad ran into a nearby bush and was heard to be violently sick.

'The body must have been here for nearly three weeks and is not in a very good state of preservation,' said Ravenscroft, pushing aside his revulsion and attempting to adopt a matter-off-act manner.

'No wonder he was at the bottom of the pond, his pockets seem to be filled with a number of heavy stones,' remarked Crabb.

'I've never seen such a thing before,' added Muncaster taking a step back.

'Then let us hope, Mr Muncaster, that you never have to witness such a scene as this ever again,' said Ravenscroft. 'Mansfield, can you identify these clothes?'

'Ye, sir. Those are the master's riding coat and breeches,' replied the butler, clearing his throat and appearing visibly shaken as he viewed the body from a distance.

'Then we are all certain that this is, was, Mr Simon Cleaves?' asked Ravenscroft as several of the farmhands gathered round.

'That's Master and no mistake,' spoke up one of the men, who had been conducting the search, after a few moments had elapsed.

'Master Simon,' pronounced another of the farm labourers, as several of his companions nodded their heads in confirmation.

'Crabb, get a blanket or some other covering from the cart,' instructed Ravenscroft anxious to hide the decomposing remains from public view.

'Yes, sir,' replied Crabb, relieved to be turning away from the scene as he walked over to the cart.

'This is a bad business, Ravenscroft,' muttered a shaken Webster.

'Indeed so, sir.'

Crabb returned with a horse blanket and draped it across the corpse.

'Thank you all for your assistance, gentlemen,' said Ravenscroft, addressing the group of men. 'It is a sad day for all of us. I would ask one more thing of you: would some of you step forward and carefully wrap Mr Simon in the blanket and then carry the body over to the cart?'

The men looked at one another uneasily.

'Well, Brothers, we can't leave the master all alone here. That wouldn't be right,' said one of the men eventually.

'Ah, ah,' said one or two of the group.

Ravenscroft stepped back as several of the men wrapped the corpse in the blanket, before carrying it across to the wagon.

'I am sorry, Mr Webster, that you had to witness such a distressing scene,' said Ravenscroft with a heavy heart, wishing that his intuition had been proved wrong.

Webster did not reply as he stared out across the pond towards the folly.

The cart began its slow progress back towards the manor house, across the fields and along the ridgeway, the farm labourers carrying their poles and nets walking on behind, closely followed silently by the five men on foot, each with his own thoughts and fears, and with Crabb bringing up the rear driving the trap at a discreet distance behind.

* * *

Later that day Ravenscroft sat alone in the inner room of the police station in Upton, turning over the dramatic events of the afternoon in his mind.

Now that they had recovered the body of Simon Cleaves from the pond at Mathon, the mystery of the whereabouts of the young landowner had at last been solved. The state of the corpse had confirmed his suspicions that Cleaves had followed his sister to the folly that morning, where he had confronted her lover, and where he had met his death either by accident, or by a deliberate act of murder, before his pockets had been filled with stones, ensuring that his weighted body would sink to the bottom, where it had remained for over three weeks.

But although one mystery had been solved it had now created others. Who had met Anne Cleaves at the folly that morning? Who had killed Simon Cleaves and consigned his body to the deep? Had Anne Cleaves been a party to the deed, or had her brother confronted his killer after she had left the scene? Most likely Anne had witnessed the death of her brother, but if that was so, why had she not spoken out? Why had she shielded her lover? Anne had always seemed pale and disturbed when questioned by Ravenscroft; now he knew the reason for her unease. Perhaps it had been Anne Cleaves herself who had killed her brother in a fit of anger, or in an attempt to protect her lover? Either way she had paid for her silence, and her involvement in the crime, with her life.

There remained the deepest mystery of all: why had the schoolmaster, John Smith, been killed, and why had certain of Simon Cleaves's possessions then been planted on his body to lead everyone to believe that it was Simon Cleaves who died in that field by the river in Upton some two weeks later? Everyone had thought that they were attending the funeral of the young landowner, and had the burial service proceeded to its conclusion, without incident, then John Smith would have taken Simon Cleaves's place in the family plot, and the real Simon Cleaves would have remained there at the bottom of the pond, lying undiscovered and slowly decomposing into nothing. It did not make any sense at all. People disappeared every day, Ravenscroft told himself, and without any apparent reason, and many would never be found ever again. Why had Anne Cleaves and her lover felt the need to kill John Smith? Why did Anne Cleave not just continue with her story about the brother who rode out one morning, and was never seen again? He could see no logical reason why they had gone on to kill the schoolmaster.

Simon Cleaves killed and consigned to the bottom of a murky pond three weeks ago; John Smith found dead in a field in Upton one week ago; Anne Cleaves cruelly murdered in her bedroom just two days previously — three bodies all linked to one killer, the mysterious lover of the mistress of Mathon Manor. But who was this man? Stapleford seemed the obvious suspect. He had attended Anne Cleaves on several occasions during the previous few weeks. Forced to resign his position at Bart's because of improper conduct, he had then been responsible for the 'resurrection' of the bodies of his former patients Sally Owens and Oliver Thompson, and had a strong association with the Thexton brothers who had transported Anne Cleaves's body to his house near Upton. This was the man who had locked him and Crabb in the cellar and who was now wanted throughout the land — but was he also a killer?

Was Gervase Webster the lover of his distant cousin? He had certainly been unwilling to assist Ravenscroft with his inquiries in the early days of his investigation, and had even been openly hostile during his visit to London. Had he been Anne Cleaves's lover, surely her brother Simon would have not reacted so violently against such a match, unless of course there was some dark secret about the family that still needed to be unearthed? Did Webster stand to inherit the estate now that his two cousins were dead and, if so, could that have been the motive for the killings? There was something about the lawyer that Ravenscroft disliked, and he was sure that Webster was still withholding some vital piece of information regarding the case.

Then there was Glenforest. He knew that Anne Cleaves had visited the school in order to see whether it was a suitable establishment for the local educational endowments, but had there been more than one visit, and had there been opportunities for her to form a close relationship with someone there? If so, that person could have been Smith, but he was now dead, so that left Smeaton or Choke. Horace Smeaton the awkward, bumbling, unappealing headmaster of Glenforest seemed a most unlikely match, but what about Marcus Choke, the humble schoolmaster and friend of Smith? Quiet and unassuming, educated and considerate, he might have possessed the qualities that she would have found attractive. He felt there was more to learn about the school and its teachers that seemed to merit further investigation.

Finally there was the mysterious woman, Rosemary, who had written so earnestly to John Smith urging him to join her at the Feathers in Ludlow, but when he and Crabb had visited the Shropshire town there appeared to be no trace of the stranger. Had she been used by Anne Cleaves and her lover to entice Smith into leaving Glenforest, so that he could then be killed? If so, it was no wonder that this unknown woman had disappeared from view. But then the more he thought about this possibility, the more it seemed that perhaps the woman had never existed at all.

'The doctor has carried out his post-mortem,' said Crabb, entering the room and breaking into Ravenscroft's thoughts. 'Not that there was much of the corpse left for him to examine.'

'And what was the result?'

'There were no bullets found in the body, so Simon Cleaves was either strangled or hit on the head before he was thrown into the pond.'

'Much as we expected,' muttered Ravenscroft. 'Did you notice, Tom, that the deceased was not wearing his waistcoat, and that when we examined Smith's body we thought that he was wearing a waistcoat that was too large for him?'

'Yes, sir, so whoever killed Simon Cleaves must have removed his waistcoat as well as his personal possessions in order that they could plant them later on Smith,'

'Exactly!'

'Mr Webster has expressed a wish that his cousins be buried together as soon as possible. I believe the funerals have been arranged for the day after tomorrow,' added Crabb.

'That seems very sensible. I wonder how Lady Cleaves will take all of this; to lose her niece must have been particularly hard to countenance, I cannot think how the loss of her nephew must be affecting her.'

'So now there are three bodies,' said Crabb.

'And three murders for us to solve, but however much I consider all the facts I find I am no nearer to identifying the killer. Is there any news of Stapleford?'

'No, sir, there have been no reports of any arrest that matches his description.'

'Well, it is no good sitting here all afternoon, Crabb. There are still a few hours of daylight left in the day. I thought we might return to Glenforest Preparatory School. We know that Anne Cleaves visited there in the weeks before her death. I want to know more of what took place during her visit. Where is Hoskings?'

'Here, sir,' said the constable quickly entering the room.

'While we are away, Hoskings, I want you to go over to the Plough and check out the Thextons' alibi. We know what Constable Crabb and I saw that night, but we are duty bound to see if their account stands up, although I think I know what the result will be.'

'Yes, sir,' replied Hoskings.

'Then you can go home. Right, Tom, bring round the trap and we will journey across to Glenforest. We should get there before nightfall.'

* * *

It was early evening when the two policemen climbed down from their trap outside Glenforest Preparatory School and, as Ravenscroft looked up at the tall, grey uninviting building and then out across towards the wild untamed common, he recalled his own schooldays when he had attended the small village school in his own community, where he had once been told by his elderly teacher there that he 'would do no good in this world', but where his own determination had led him onwards to prove her wrong. Eventually he secured a scholarship to the nearby grammar school, giving him the confidence and education to join the police force in London all those many years ago.

'A penny for your thoughts, sir,' remarked Crabb, about to ring the bell at the side of the main door.

'Oh, I was just remembering my own schooldays,' smiled Ravenscroft.

'It was the village school for me. None of this fancy private education. My parents could never afford it, and even if they could, it would have done me no good,' said Crabb.

'Good day. Welcome, gentlemen. Ah, it is Inspector Ravenswood if I am not mistaken,' said Smeaton opening the door and giving a broad smile that displayed his large upper teeth to their full effect.

'Ravenscroft. I do not believe you have met my associate Constable Crabb.'

'Ah, yes, but I see you are not here today concerning the education of your son, Master . . . er—'

'Richard, and yes you are correct in your assumption, Mr Smeaton. I have come to ask you some more questions about the case we are investigating,' said Ravenscroft.

'I think I have told you everything I knew about poor John Smith,' said Smeaton, squinting through his misty spectacles at the two policemen.

'It is not Mr Smith that I am seeking information about. It is Miss Anne Cleaves who concerns me.'

'Miss Cleaves? Whatever can I tell you about her? Nothing much to tell, I can assure you, but I can see that you are in earnest, my dear sir, so perhaps you had better come inside,' said Smeaton opening the door wider.

The two detectives followed the headmaster along the passageway and inner hall, and into Smeaton's office, Crabb casting curious glances at the many photographs of masters and boys that hung on the walls.

'Now then, Inspector, please do take a seat — and you as well, Constable Cribb,' said Smeaton indicating two chairs placed before an untidy desk.

'Crabb,' corrected the policeman.

'Yes, of course you are. Crabb. What an unusual name. Well, do take a seat, Constable.'

'Mr Smeaton, I recall on my last visit here that you said that Miss Cleaves had visited the school to discuss the possible admission of certain boys from the village of Mathon,' began Ravenscroft, seating himself.

'That is correct. What an excellent memory you have,' smiled Smeaton brushing aside a pile of papers on his desk.

'I wonder if you could tell me in detail what transpired during her visit.'

'Well . . . er . . . Miss Cleaves spoke of her intention to send some of the village boys here, and I informed her of the education our children receive in this establishment. Then the good lady expressed an interest in looking around the school.'

'Do go on,' encouraged Ravenscroft.

'Well . . . er . . . that was all really. I remember we visited a number of the classrooms. Miss Cleaves particularly wished to see both the boys' sleeping quarters and the kitchens as well, of course, but I was unable personally to show her all of those,' said Smeaton, leaning back in his chair, and cupping his hands as he stared up at the ceiling.

'Oh, why was that, Mr Smeaton?' asked Ravenscroft.

'Why was what?' replied Smeaton puzzled.

'Why were you unable to show Miss Cleaves around the school?'

'Dear, did I say that? Yes, of course I did. Yes, I remember now. Another parent suddenly arrived without any warning and requested my urgent and undivided attention regarding an unfortunate injury which his son had just sustained playing rugby that morning. So I am afraid I had to leave Miss Cleaves in the capable hands of Mr Choke. Yes, that was it. Fortunately Mr Choke was not teaching at that moment, so he was able to step into the breach, as it were.'

'I see. How long did Miss Cleaves stay during her visit?' asked Ravenscroft, curious to know more about what had taken place.

'I believe she left probably about ten minutes after Marcus began to show her around the school.'

'Tell me, did Miss Cleaves return after that initial visit?'

'Well . . . er . . . I think she may have done, about five weeks ago, I believe,' answered Smeaton.

'But you are not certain? Is that because you did not see Miss Cleaves yourself on this second visit?'

'Yes, you have it exactly, my dear sir. I remember I was out visiting Worcester that day, and I believe the good lady must have called unannounced, and so Mr Choke must have seen her. Yes, that was it,' said Smeaton with a degree of triumph.

'How did you know that Miss Cleaves called this second time if you were not here at the time?'

'Ah yes, how? Ah yes, because the housekeeper mentioned it.'

'Not Mr Choke himself?'

'No, I do not believe so. But I remember Choke telling me all about the visit when I asked him. It seemed that Miss Cleaves just wanted another look around the school before arriving at her decision as to whether to send the boys here or not.'

'And what was that decision, Mr Smeaton?'

'Well, that is the curious thing. I have not heard from the good lady since. Most curious, but then I suppose these things do take a time to be resolved. Forgive me, Inspector, but I do not quite see the point of all these questions,' said the headmaster leaning forward across the desk and wrinkling his nose as he stared intently at Ravenscroft.

'I have to ask these questions, Mr Smeaton, because I am afraid I have to inform you that Miss Cleaves is dead,' announced Ravenscroft.

'Dead! My dear me! What a terrible thing to have happened. The poor lady looked in the goodness of health when she visited here, although on reflection she did seem rather pale, if I remember.'

'She was murdered,' said Crabb.

'Murdered! Murdered? Good gracious. What a terrible thing to have happened,' repeated Smeaton shocked.

'So you can see why we need to know all we can about Miss Cleaves and what she was doing in the weeks leading up to her death,' said Ravenscroft.

'Yes, yes, absolutely, of course, Inspector, and if I can help you in anyway then please do not hesitate to ask,' said Smeaton.

'Thank you. You already have. Tell me, Mr Smeaton, have you ever had occasion to visit Mathon Manor?'

'No,' answered the perplexed headmaster.

'And you have never met Mr Simon Cleaves?'

'No.'

'Well, thank you for your time, Mr Smeaton. I wonder if we might have a word with Mr Choke before we take our leave?' asked Ravenscroft, rising from his seat.

'Yes, of course. I think Marcus is in the library at present. I saw him in there a few moments before your arrival.'

'Thank you.'

'If you would care to follow me, gentlemen,' said Smeaton, leading the way deeper into the house, before opening a door at the end of the corridor.

Ravenscroft and Crabb entered the library and saw that Choke was seated at the table reading a large book.

'Ah, Choke, you may recall Inspector . . . er—'

'Ravenscroft,' provided the detective.

'Yes, Inspector Ravenscroft. He has some more questions for you,' said Smeaton.

'Good day to you, Inspector,' said the schoolmaster, rising from his chair.

'Mr Choke,' acknowledged Ravenscroft. 'Thank you, Mr Smeaton, you have been most helpful.'

'Yes, yes, of course. Well, I will leave you in the capable hands of Mr Choke,' said Smeaton offering a brief smile before leaving the room.

'You have some news about poor John and the lady who wrote to him from Ludlow?' enquired Choke, earnestly.

'We have not been able to find out anything else regarding your friend and associate Mr Smith, and our visit to Ludlow proved rather futile,' answered Ravenscroft.

'Oh, why was that, Inspector?'

'None at the Feathers had heard of the mysterious Rosemary, and our enquiries in the town only established that no one of that name had recently arrived there.'

'Oh dear,' sympathized Choke.

'But it is not Mr Smith who is our main concern today, but Miss Anne Cleaves, and I think you may be able to assist us with that.'

'I will do all that I can to help of course, but I am not sure that I can provide you with any information regarding that lady.'

'We understand that on her visit to the school to discuss the possible scholarships for the local boys, you showed her around the classrooms and dormitories?' asked Ravenscroft.

'Yes, that was indeed so. Unfortunately Mr Smeaton was forced to attend to another parent, if I recall.'

'Can you tell me what you and Miss Cleaves spoke about?'

'Nothing in particular. As I said, I showed her around the rest of the school and explained the system of education we have here. I remember that she was most interested in all that I had to tell her. I only wish that some of the parents expressed that amount of concern. She was particularly interested in the display we have concerning the raising of funds for the poor children of Sierra Leone.'

'Oh? That is rather unusual,' remarked Ravenscroft.

'Not really, the idea for such enterprise was my suggestion. I am very interested in the work of the Church Missionary Society, and have given a great deal of thought to the idea that I might one day even resign my position here to go and help the needy of that country,' said Choke.

'We understand that Miss Cleaves returned to the school on a second occasion.'

'Yes, that is indeed so.'

'Mr Smeaton was absent upon that occasion?'

'Yes.'

'So you attended upon Miss Cleaves?'

'Yes. Miss Cleaves wanted to pay a second visit to the school before making a decision regarding the children of her village, but she also wanted to know more about the poor children of Sierra Leone,' smiled Choke. 'She was very enthusiastic about my interest, and asked how she might be of assistance to me.'

'I see, and what did you say to Miss Cleaves?'

'I told her that I would like to go to Africa as a teacher and missionary, to help the poor children there, but that I felt I was unable to do that.'

'Oh, why was that, sir?' asked Crabb.

'I am a comparatively poor man, and if I were to go now I would have little in the way to contribute, financially, to my work over there. It was, is, my dream to build a large school there which would be open to all children irrespective of their race, creed or educational background.'

'A very noble enterprise — and what did Miss Cleaves say about your "dream" Mr Choke?'

'She said that it was a good Christian thing to want to aspire to, and that she would do all she could to help me achieve this endeavour.'

'She offered financial support?' asked a Ravenscroft curiously.

'I believe she might have done, I rather hoped so, but, of course, she did not commit herself one way or the other. She said she would go away and think very carefully about what I had said.'

'Have you spoken to Miss Cleaves since that day, or received any communication from her?'

'No. I had thought that rather strange, but then I came to the conclusion that I had perhaps spoken out of turn, and had been somewhat too zealous in the outlining of my case, and that the good lady had forgotten our conversation.'

'I see,' said Ravenscroft.

'But I fear the worst has happened,' said Choke suddenly with alarm. 'You would not be asking me all these questions if something dreadful had not happened to Miss Cleaves.'

'I am afraid you are correct, Mr Choke. Later on in the day when we last spoke to you, Miss Cleaves was cruelly murdered in her bedroom at Mathon Manor,' announced Ravenscroft, closely watching the schoolmaster's reaction to his words.

'Miss Cleaves? Murdered? It cannot be so,' replied Choke burying his face in his hands.

'I am sorry to be the bearer of such bad news,' said Ravenscroft after several moments of silence had passed.

'How can this be so? The poor Christian soul, struck down so;' said Choke, looking up and staring at Ravenscroft, the colour draining away from his face. 'How can this be?' Who can have done such a terrible thing?'

'We do not know at present, but we do believe that the person who killed Miss Cleaves was engaged in a romantic relationship with her, and that several letters written to her by this person were also taken. I have to ask you, Mr Choke, did you ever write to Miss Cleaves or see her again after her visit here?'

'No, no. I have told you that that was the last time I saw Miss Cleaves.'

'You have never visited Mathon Manor, sir?' asked Crabb.

'No, Constable. Never,'

'We have also recovered the body of Miss Cleaves's brother, Mr. Simon Cleaves, from a nearby pond. He had been dead for three weeks,' continued Ravenscroft.

'This is dreadful! Perfectly dreadful,' said the schoolmaster distraught.

'You never met Mr Cleaves?' continued Ravenscroft with his questioning.

'No. No. Who can have committed these dreadful deeds?'

'That is what we are endeavouring to find out, Mr Choke. Did Mr Smith ever mention to you anything at all concerning the Cleaves family?'

'No, I believe not,' replied the schoolmaster after some deliberation.

'Thank you, Mr Choke. You have been most helpful in answering our questions. I am only sorry that we have had to impart such bad news to you. We will take our leave now.'

'All this has come as rather a shock. I have a few pounds, not much as I am sure you can appreciate, but if I could offer some reward leading to the arrest of the perpetrator of these evil acts. . .' said Choke, his voice trailing away as he turned round and looked sorrowfully through the library window.

'That will not be necessary, Mr Choke. I wish you good evening.'

* * *

'Well, Tom, what do you make of our schoolmaster Marcus Choke?' asked Ravenscroft as the trap made its way along the darkening lanes towards Ledbury.

'He seemed quite distraught when you told him the news about Miss Cleaves,' said Crabb.

'Yes. On the surface he appears to be quite a noble fellow, at first offering to pay for John Smith's funeral, and now with his philanthropic aspirations in distant Sierra Leone.'

'He even offered to put up a reward for the apprehension of Anne Cleaves's killer.'

'Yes, I thought that was somewhat unusual, considering that he claims he is not in possession of funds, but then perhaps it was just an impulsive gesture, or the reward offered was quite small. I suppose his heart is in the right place. Nevertheless there is something that worries me. Smeaton said that it was the housekeeper who told him about Anne Cleaves's second visit to the school. You would have thought that Choke would have mentioned it to him first. Was the real reason for Anne Cleaves's visit to see Choke, rather than to view the school again? We only have Choke's word for it that they talked about his missionary aspirations in Africa, whereas in fact their conversation could have been along quite different lines.'

'You think that Choke could have killed Anne and Simon Cleaves?' asked Crabb.

'I don't honestly know. I would certainly like to know a lot more though about Marcus Choke before I can answer that question. He and Anne Cleaves could well have been lovers, and the whole story about missionary work in Africa could be a complete fabrication. Either Choke is an honest God-fearing fellow, or a very cunning rogue.'

'I think we can discount Horace Smeaton as a suspect. I cannot see a sophisticated lady like Anne Cleaves taking up with such an ugly man as that.'

'Yes, I'm inclined to agree with you, Tom. I don't think Horace Smeaton is our killer. The man would not have the ability to swat a fly in a teacup, let alone kill three people — but, then, appearances can sometimes be deceptive. Anyway, home now. Let us see what tomorrow brings.'

CHAPTER TEN

LEDBURY AND UPTON-UPON-SEVERN

'We have him, sir!' announced a triumphant Hoskings as Ravenscroft and Crabb entered the police station the following morning.

'Who do you have precisely, Hoskings?' asked Ravenscroft still feeling somewhat jaded after the events of the previous day.

'Him sir; you know, the one we are after. That mad doctor.'

'Stapleford?'

'Yes, sir.'

'Well man, where is he?'

'He is in the cells, sir. One or two of our men in Stow-on-the-Wold recognized him as he was changing horses at one of the inns there, so they arrested him and bought him back here early this morning,' continued Hoskings, enthusiastically.

'Splendid news, Hoskings; bring him into the office straight away. Did you give him some refreshment when he arrived?' asked a more cheerful Ravenscroft.

'Yes, sir.'

Ravenscroft and Crabb went into the inner office, as Hoskings left for the cells.

'Well, Tom, this is good news indeed. Now perhaps we can get to the bottom of this case,' said Ravenscroft seating himself behind the small table.

'Let us hope so, sir,' added Crabb.

'Make sure you keep notes, Tom,' instructed Ravenscroft, laying out paper and pencil before him.

The door opened and Hoskings entered, holding an unkempt and angry-looking Stapleford by the arm.

'I think you can take the cuffs off the prisoner, Constable Hoskings,' instructed Ravenscroft. 'Take a seat, Doctor.'

Hoskings unlocked the handcuffs as Stapleford sat down on the chair facing Ravenscroft.

'Thank you, Hoskings, you may go. So, Dr Stapleford, that was a rather foolish thing you did the other night. You must have known that it would have only been a short time before my constables came looking for me, and that you would not have gone far before you were recognized and arrested,' began Ravenscroft.

Stapleford said nothing and, after he had glared briefly in the detective's direction, he stared down at his clasped hands on the table in front of him.

'Well, Stapleford, where shall we begin? Preventing a police officer from carrying out his duties, or shall it be imprisoning police officers in that ghastly dissecting theatre of yours? Or will it be the abduction of a dead corpse, or perhaps it should be the resurrection of the remains of Sally Owens and Oliver Thomson? Then there is the murder of Simon Cleaves, Miss Anne Cleaves and—'

'I have murdered no one!' interrupted Stapleford angrily.

'The evidence suggests otherwise.'

'What evidence? You have no evidence to use against me.'

'We know that you saw Miss Cleaves a number of times in the weeks leading up to her death.'

'In a professional capacity, man,' growled Stapleford.

'So you were not her lover?'

'Good grief, how can you even think such a thing?'

'Then perhaps you would enlighten us as to the nature of your visits?' asked Ravenscroft, leaning back in his chair and studying his suspect closely.

'What took place between Miss Cleaves and I was an entirely confidential matter, and is of no concern to you or anyone else,' snapped Stapleford.

'May I remind you, Dr Stapleford, that Miss Cleaves is now dead, having been brutally murdered in her own bedroom, and that you are now our chief suspect. The sooner you tell us everything the better it may be for you,' said Ravenscroft firmly.

'All right, all right, man, Miss Cleaves was suffering from a debilitating illness. She was far from well. To put it bluntly, she was fading away. All I could do was to prescribe a number of medicines that I believed would arrest her decline.'

'You mean Fowler's Solution and Valentine's Beef Juice,' interrupted Ravenscroft.

'Yes, those certainly were prescribed, amongst other medicines.'

'Can you explain to us why Miss Cleaves was in this condition?'

'No. Some conditions are unexplainable; they just occur. Sometimes the patient recovers; on other occasions we can do little to help,' answered Stapleford.

'And which do you think was the case this time?' asked Ravenscroft, unsure as to whether the doctor was telling him the truth, or not.

'I had hopes that Miss Cleaves would make a recovery, given time. Certainly in the last two weeks before her death she seemed to rally somewhat, despite the anxiety over her brother's disappearance.'

'Did Mr Simon Cleaves approve of your visits?'

'I believe so. He was never at the Manor when I called.'

'So you never actually met Mr Cleaves?' asked Ravenscroft.

'That is indeed so.'

'You told us when we first interviewed you that you had no knowledge of the Cleaves family, and yet you issued a death certificate for Mr Cleaves when you examined the dead man at Upton. I find that rather strange, don't you?'

'I said I had never met Mr Cleaves; I only visited Miss Cleaves,' replied Stapleford emphatically.

'Where did these medical consultations usually take place?'

'In the drawing room,' answered Stapleford.

'We understand that on two occasions two of these so-called "consultations" took place in the privacy of Miss Cleaves's bedroom.'

'Yes, that may have been so. I needed to examine my patient, and the lady's bedroom would have been a more suitable place to carry out such medical procedure, than in a drawing room where one might have been disturbed at any moment,' replied Stapleford in a matter-of-fact tone of voice.

'In such situations would it not have been more prudent if a maid had been present at such examinations?' suggested Ravenscroft.

'Miss Cleaves did not request the presence of her maid.'

'Oh, why was that?'

'She was anxious that no one in the house should be aware of her condition. She did not want to worry Lady Cleaves.'

'And yet you say that her brother was aware that his sister was ill, and that he approved of your visits. That would seem to contradict what you have just said.'

'Mr Cleaves was certainly aware of my initial visit, after that he was not usually there when I called.'

'How very convenient,' said Ravenscroft allowing himself the briefest of smiles.

'What do you mean by that remark?' glowered Stapleford.

'I do not mean anything by it.'

'Look, Ravenscroft, you asked me about the nature of my visits to Miss Cleaves, and I have told you. If you choose not to believe what I have told you, or suggest that some kind of impropriety took place during these visits, then that is your concern. My conscience is clear.'

'Oh I doubt that very much, Dr Stapleford. I think you have a great deal to answer for. Tell me about Oliver Thompson. He was one of your patients, I believe?' said Ravenscroft, deciding to alter his line of questioning.

'He was. He died, unfortunately, at a very young age. There was nothing I could do for him.'

'Why did you resurrect his body?'

'"Resurrect his body?" What a quaint turn of phrase. That is complete nonsense.'

'We know that the grave was disturbed shortly after his burial. Were you anxious to acquire his body so that you could dissect it for medical research?'

'Certainly not,' protested Stapleford.

'Sally Owens, what about her? She was another patient of yours whose grave was disturbed shortly after her burial.'

'Now look here, Ravenscroft, all this is complete nonsense.'

'I don't think so. I think that if I apply for an exhumation order, and we open the two coffins we would find nothing inside. I believe you took those bodies from the graveyard, here in Upton, and that you then dissected the bodies for your own macabre ends,' said Ravenscroft forcibly.

'Nonsense; this is all nonsense. But why don't you just do that then, Ravenscroft? Get your exhumation order. You will be made to look a fool, and even if you were to find the coffins empty, you would still have no evidence to prove that they are in my collection,' retorted Stapleford, raising his voice.

'How many other bodies did the Thextons supply you with?' persisted Ravenscroft. 'We know that you could not acquire the bodies of Sally Owens and Oliver Thompson directly from the Thextons, because the two families of deceased used other undertakers in the area. That is why you had to act on your own and acquire the bodies from the churchyard on your own initiative. But, I repeat, how many more victims were passed directly onto you by the Thextons?' said Ravenscroft, more and more angry by the answers given by the medical practitioner.

'I refuse to answer these unfounded accusations,' smirked Stapleford sitting back in his chair.

'Then perhaps you could tell us why the Thextons delivered Miss Cleaves's body to your house.'

'I wanted to carry out a number of medical tests on the body.'

'Oh come now, Stapleford, that is unbelievable.'

'Believe it or not, that is the truth. I asked Shortcross and Maudlin to let me have the body for a few hours so that I could conduct some important medical tests, and I arranged with them to collect the body from the house the following morning.'

'That is not what the Thextons told us. They claim that they were drinking in the Plough all night here in Upton,'

'Then they are lying.'

'You and I, Dr Stapleford, know that they are lying, because they were seen delivering poor Anne Cleaves's corpse to your house. What were these so-called medical tests that you wished to carry out?' asked Ravenscroft.

'As I have just told you, Miss Cleaves was dying from a strange, unknown illness. I wanted to know what had caused that illness, so that others might be able to live in the future,' retorted Stapleford, with added confidence.

'That is very philanthropic, Doctor, but I must say I don't believe a word of it. Why did you decide to lock us in that underground room and then seek to escape if that was the case?' asked Ravenscroft, frustrated by his lack of progress.

'Because I knew that if I told you the truth you would jump to the wrong conclusion. People are so narrow minded, squeamish and prejudiced when it comes to medical research.'

Ravenscroft leaned back in his chair and closely scrutinized his suspect. It seemed to him that his adversary had an answer for everything, no matter which line of questioning he adopted, and he was aware that he was in danger of losing the initiative. Stapleford's arrogance and confidence had annoyed him, and he knew that if the case ever got to court it would not hold up well to cross examination.

'Did you kill Simon Cleaves?' he asked, confronting his opponent once more.

'No, of course not; why would I want to kill Simon Cleaves?'

'We recovered his body from the pond near the folly out at Mathon. He had been brutally murdered. You don't seem surprised by the news.'

'I knew you were searching for him after all that mix up with the burial and, as he had not appeared, it seems logical to me that he would be dead already, but I will repeat what I have just said: I did not kill either Simon or Anne Cleaves, or anyone else for that matter. You have no evidence against me, so I suggest you release me now.'

'We may not have the evidence yet, Stapleford, but it will only be a matter of time, I can assure you. All murderers eventually give themselves away in one way or the other. In the meantime we will be holding you in custody until the date of your trial has been arranged,' said Ravenscroft leaning forward and staring directly at his suspect.

'On what charge?' demanded Stapleford.

'Stealing a body for an unlawful act, obstructing and imprisoning police officers in the lawful pursuit of their duties; that will do for a start. I am sure that when we take a closer look at your medical specimens we can then add a few more charges. You will be going down for a very long time. I do not think that even the illustrious Sefton Rawlinson will consider it worthwhile taking up your hopeless case,' said Ravenscroft firmly.

'Hoskings! Hoskings!'

'Yes, sir,' said the policeman opening the door quickly, and entering the room.

'Put the cuffs back on the prisoner and then take him back to the cells,' instructed Ravenscroft.

'Yes, sir,' replied Hoskings.

'You will regret this, Ravenscroft, I promise you,' said Stapleford, rising from his seat angrily.

'I do not take kindly to threats from men like you. Take him away, Hoskings.'

Stapleford glared at Ravenscroft before the policeman ushered him from the room.

'He was as slippery as an eel caught from the River Severn,' remarked Crabb, once the two men were alone.

'Yes, but he is quite correct when he says that we have no evidence to bring against him for the murders of Simon and Anne Cleaves, and John Smith.'

'You still think that he did, it sir?'

'Strangely enough, I don't believe that he is our man. Of course we only have his word for it that he was treating Anne Cleaves, and that she was dying from some unknown complaint. That would certainly explain her pale and languid demeanour, but it could all be lies, and he could have been her lover after all,' said Ravenscroft thinking out loud. 'I am convinced however that he procured Anne Cleaves's body with the intention of dissecting it for his so-called medical experiments, and I am sure that he also acquired the bodies of Sally Owens and Oliver Thompson for the same reason. I am also confident that there must have been others as well.'

'That should be enough to either send him to the gallows, or imprison him for the rest of his days,' suggested Crabb.

'One would hope so. I think we should certainly apply for an exhumation order to open those coffins. We should also bring in those Thexton brothers. They are certainly involved in all this. Perhaps after another night in the cells, Stapleford might lose some of his arrogance and we might persuade him to implicate the undertakers. However, none of this is helping us to discover who murdered our three victims. Do you know, Tom, that the more I think about this case, the more I cannot comprehend why the schoolmaster was killed after Simon Cleaves's death, and why it was made to look as though it was Cleaves who was found dead by the river.'

'I've locked him in the cells, sir,' said Hoskings re-entering the room.

'Excellent. Now, Hoskings, I presume that you made enquiries at the Plough regarding the Thextons?' asked Ravenscroft.

'Yes, sir. One or two of the old regulars can't remember who was there that night whereas the rest all swear blind that all three of the Thexton brothers were there all evening till nearly twelve.'

'Just as we thought,' smiled Crabb.

'Now, Hoskings, I want you to send this telegram as soon as possible. It is addressed to Scotland Yard in London. I want to see if they have any information in their records concerning Marcus Choke,' said Ravenscroft, hastily writing out a note, before handing it to the policeman. 'There you are.'

'Yes, sir,' said the constable, taking the sheet of paper before searching in the inside pocket of his tunic. 'Oh, sir, I nearly forgot, this telegram arrived for you when you were interviewing the prisoner.'

Ravenscroft tore open the envelope. 'It's from Anthony Midwinter in Ledbury.' He read aloud:

HAVE JUST LEARNED OF SIMON CLEAVES DEATH STOP IMPERATIVE I TALK WITH YOU AS SOON AS POSSIBLE STOP MOST URGENT STOP MIDWINTER

'I wonder what he wants?' asked Crabb.

'Of course. While we have been chasing round in circles we have ignored the most obvious line of inquiry!' exclaimed Ravenscroft. 'Tom, why was Anthony Midwinter at the funeral?'

'It must have been out of respect for the family.'

'Exactly! Midwinter must be the Cleaves family solicitor. That was why he was attending the funeral. We should have asked him about the affairs of the family, and Gervase Webster. Come, we don't have a moment to lose.'

* * *

They left the medieval half-timbered market building in Ledbury behind them, crossed over the busy main road, and walked the few yards up the Homend towards the offices of Midwinter, Oliphant and Burrows, Solicitors.

As the detectives entered the office, a clerk rose from his seat. 'Ah, Mr Ravenscroft, Mr Midwinter is expecting you, sir.'

'Thank you.'

The clerk tapped gently on the door of the inner office. 'There is Inspector Ravenscroft to see you, sir.'

'Ah, Ravenscroft, so good of you to come,' said Midwinter, rising from his chair and coming forward eagerly to meet the two men.

'Mr Midwinter. We came as soon as we received your telegram,' said Ravenscroft.

'This is such terrible news. Poor Mr Cleaves. They say that he was found dead in the pond near the Folly. Murdered they say!' said a worried Midwinter.

'News travels fast,' remarked Ravenscroft, accepting the seat that the solicitor offered. 'But you are correct, Mr Midwinter, when you say that he was murdered. We also believe that Simon Cleaves had been dead in the water for at least three weeks.'

'Terrible! This is terrible. First it was that poor schoolmaster, then Miss Cleaves, and now poor Simon Cleaves. This is all quite terrible. What a situation we find ourselves in.'

'Indeed. Your message implied that you wished to talk to us as a matter of urgency,' said Ravenscroft.

'Ah yes, as soon as I heard the news, I knew that you would want to know as soon as possible,' said Midwinter seating himself behind his desk.

Ravenscroft gave the solicitor a look of encouragement.

'Yes, now, where is it,' said Midwinter, searching through a pile of old documents on his desk. 'Ah, here we are. It is all a question of wills, you see.'

'I thought it might be,' said Ravenscroft. 'You are, of course, referring to Mr Simon Cleaves's will.'

'Oh no, not that will, rather old Martin Cleaves's will.'

'Go on,' said Ravenscroft anxious to know more about this unexpected line of development.

'Martin Cleaves, as you are probably aware, was the father of both Miss Anne and Master Simon. He and his wife both died within six months of each other some eleven years ago, when the children were aged twelve and fourteen respectively,' continued Midwinter, opening out a large document and spreading it out before him on the table. 'A year before he died, he sat in that very same chair that you are now sitting in, Mr Ravenscroft, and instructed me to draw up his last will and testament. His main concern was that he should provide for his two young children in the event of his untimely death, but at the same time he was anxious that Simon should not acquire the estate until he had attained the age of twenty-five. The will placed the estate of Mathon Manor, with all its lands and possessions, in trust, for the children, until that date of maturity. Their aunt, Lady Cleaves, was to have supervision of the children and the trust until that date.'

'So what you are saying, Mr Midwinter, if I have understood you correctly, is that Simon Cleaves did not stand to inherit the estate until his twenty-fifth birthday?' asked Ravenscroft.

'That is indeed so.'

'What age was Simon Cleaves when he died?' asked Ravenscroft leaning forward in his chair.

'Ah, well, now that is the interesting thing. Simon Cleaves would have been twenty-five on 21st March.'

'What date was John Smith's body found, Crabb?' asked Ravenscroft, turning towards his constable.

'On 25th March, sir,' replied Crabb after consulting his pocket book.

'But we now know that Simon Cleaves died much earlier in the month,' said Ravenscroft.

'Yes, sir, probably on 9th March; that was the date that he was last seen leaving the house by the servants,' added Crabb.

'This is all very interesting, Mr Midwinter. So Simon Cleaves was killed twelve days before his twenty-fifth birthday when he was due to come into his inheritance — and yet someone wanted us to believe that he died as the result of a fall from his horse, some four days after that birthday,' said Ravenscroft intently. 'Tell me, Mr Midwinter, if Simon Cleaves died before attaining the age of twenty-five what happens to the estate?'

'That is where it becomes most interesting. Mr Martin Cleaves quite clearly states, here in the will, that should his son die before the age of twenty-five, then everything is to be sold and the proceeds given to the Foundling Hospital in London "in recognition of all their good works in the past, and to provide suitable apprenticeships for the young children in the future," to quote the exact words.'

'Good Lord, so it all goes to a lot of orphans!' exclaimed Crabb.

'A very noble foundation, I think we would all agree,' said Ravenscroft. 'Was any provision made for Miss Anne?'

'Oh yes, part of the funds was to be used to purchase an annuity to provide a yearly income of one hundred and fifty pounds for the rest of her life.'

'That does not seem very much,' remarked Ravenscroft. 'I find all this very interesting and yes, somewhat amusing. It would seem that the chief beneficiaries of all this would seem to be the Foundling Hospital in London.'

'It seems unlikely that someone from that institution could have committed the crime,' remarked Crab perplexed.

'Can you tell me whether Simon Cleaves also left a will?' asked Ravenscroft. 'It would be interesting to know who would stand to inherit in the event of his death.'

'Indeed so. Mr Simon did indeed make a will, last year, in fact. He was concerned that his affairs should be put in order ready for when he inherited the estate. Now where have I put it,' said a flustered Midwinter searching through his papers.

'Someone, Crabb, wanted everyone to believe that Simon Cleaves had attained his majority, that was why the substitution of the body took place,' said Ravenscroft.

'Ah, here we are. I think it would be better if I read the exact words of the will,' said the solicitor, peering at the document intently through his spectacles. 'I bequeath Mathon Manor, the house, grounds and estate and all its possessions and monies to my sister, Anne Cleaves of Mathon Manor, once I have attained the age of twenty-five years, unless I be married by the date of my demise, in which case everything will pass to my wife and heirs accordingly, with the exception of the creation of an annuity to provide a yearly income of two hundred pounds to the said Anne Cleaves, to be paid for the rest of her life."

'So Anne Cleaves stood to inherit the estate in the event of her brother's death, but only if he was over the age of twenty-five?' said Ravenscroft.

'Precisely,' added Midwinter looking up from the document.

'So, Anne Cleaves must have killed her brother, because he was under age, and because the orphans stood to inherit, she then had to kill the schoolmaster to make it look as though her brother was still alive after his twenty-fifth birthday. It all seems very complicated,' said Crabb.

'You are correct, Tom, except that it was probably Anne Cleaves's lover who killed Simon Cleaves,' corrected Ravenscroft.

'Why didn't they just wait until he was twenty-five?' continued Crabb.

'That would have been the logical thing to have done if the murder had been pre-arranged. The fact that Cleaves was murdered beforehand indicates that it was not planned, but was rather the result of an accident or an argument. I believe that Simon Cleaves followed his sister to the Folly that morning, where he confronted her and her lover, that the two men fought together and that Cleaves was killed. The couple then disposed of the body in the pond, carefully adding rocks and stones to his pockets so that he would sink to the bottom and never be found, before deciding that they needed to kill someone else, two weeks later, to make it look as though Simon had died after inheriting the estate. It was all very neat,' pronounced Ravenscroft.

'Very baffling indeed, Inspector, so this person, who killed Simon, must have thought that he could later marry the dead man's sister and thereby inherit the estate,' suggested Midwinter.

'Indeed, but then the plan ran into difficulties. They had not anticipated that Lady Cleaves would insist on opening the coffin and, of course, once it was established that the dead man was not Simon Cleaves, and that you, Mr Midwinter, had alerted us to this state of affairs, and we had then begun to question Anne Cleaves, the murderer knew that it would only be a matter of time before the lady in question would break down and admit her role in the murder and deception. Consequently the murderer knew that he would have to kill Anne Cleaves before she incriminated him. He also had to be sure that he recovered the letters he had written to her, and that was why he arranged to meet her in secret in her bedroom,' said Ravenscroft.

'I see. I see,' repeated Midwinter.

'I am afraid that we are dealing with a very devious and unprincipled killer,' added Ravenscroft. 'I don't suppose Miss Cleaves also made a will?'

'Not that I am aware of, Inspector. If she did make a will it was not with me.'

'Of course!' exclaimed Ravenscroft. 'Gervase Webster mentioned to me that his cousin had recently visited his offices in the Temple in London. The reason for her visit must have been to make such a will.'

'That may tell us who she named as her chief beneficiary,' said Midwinter.

'And also if she named her lover,' added Crabb.

'That may be so. Mr Midwinter, thank you with providing us with this valuable information,' said Ravenscroft, standing up and about to make his departure.

'Oh, there is one other thing that I forgot to mention to you when I visited your house. The recollection has only just come back to me. At the funeral I noticed that someone was intent on watching the proceedings from outside the churchyard,' said Midwinter.

'Can you tell me more about this person?' asked Ravenscroft with interest.

'He was a man of fairly tall stature but not excessively so, wearing a long coat and hat, so I was unable to obtain a full view of him, but I do remember that he was taking a great interest in all the proceedings. When the coffin was opened, and it was revealed that it did not contain Simon Cleaves, I looked up again and noticed that the man was making a somewhat hurried exit from the scene.'

'Do you think that he was young, or elderly, in the way in which he moved?'

'I cannot be sure, but I would say he was not an old man.'

'Do you think that you would recognize him if you ever saw him again, Mr Midwinter?' asked Ravenscroft.

'I am not sure I would, or would not. He certainly did not remind me of anyone I had previously encountered,' replied the solicitor, shaking his head. 'I suppose he could have just been someone passing by, who just paused to see what was happening in the churchyard.'

'No. Mr Midwinter, I think he was more than that. I believe he was our killer. He just wanted to make sure that the burial had taken place,' answered Ravenscroft, seriously.

'Good gracious! I wish I had taken greater note of him,' sighed the solicitor. 'I am sorry that I have not been of greater assistance to you.'

'But you were not to know the future course of events at the time. On the contrary, Mr Midwinter, you have been of great assistance to us. Thank you once again.'

* * *

'Well, Tom, what do you make of all that?' asked Ravenscroft as the two policemen walked back down the Homend.

'A very cunning plan to kill the schoolmaster and make it look as though the body was that of Simon Cleaves, so that the inheritance could pass to Miss Cleaves,' answered Crabb.

'They had to find someone who was approximately the same age and appearance as Simon Cleaves, and preferably someone who appeared to be alone in the world, and who consequently would not be missed by close relatives and friends. Anne Cleaves must have remembered meeting John Smith on her visit to Glenforest, and she and her lover then had to make sure he left the school so that they could kill him and make the substitution. That is where the mysterious "Rosemary" came into the story,' said Ravenscroft.

'We don't even know whether she actually existed,' suggested Crabb.

'Whether she did or not, Smith received some communication of sorts that made him leave the school in a hurry.'

'What do we do now. sir?'

'I want to know what was in Anne Cleaves's will, and to do that we need to speak to Gervase Webster. Let us hope he is still at Mathon Manor.'

'Excuse me, sir, but is you Ravenscroft?' asked a young boy. running in front of the pair.

'Yes, I am Inspector Ravenscroft, but how did you know that?'

'Seen you around the town, I 'as. Urgent telegram for ye, sir; said to deliver it to Midwinter's, as you would probably be there,' said the boy handing over an envelope.

'Thank you,' said Ravenscroft giving the boy a silver coin. 'Good Lord, it's from Hoskings!'

'But we only left Upton two hours ago,' said Crabb, perplexed.

'*STAPLEFORD ESCAPED STOP COME AS SOON AS POSSIBLE STOP HOSKINGS,*' read Ravenscroft. 'What the devil! Here, boy, I need to send another telegram. Give me a page from your pocket book, Crabb. Now, if I write out this message for you, will you send it as soon as possible?'

'Don't know that, sir. I think you will have to fill in the form at the office,' protested the telegraph boy.

'We haven't time for that now,' replied Ravenscroft, quickly writing out the note. 'This is urgent police business. I'll give you another shilling if you do this for me, and there is the fee as well, together with the address for delivery.'

'Right you are, sir. Pleasure doing business with you, Inspector Ravenscroft,' smiled the boy, hastily taking the note and the money before running off down the street.

'What was that, sir?' asked Crabb.

'Telegram to Webster at Mathon Court asking him to send a summary of Anne Cleaves's will as soon as possible over to the station in Upton, which is where we are going now to see why Hoskings has let Stapleford escape!'

CHAPTER ELEVEN

UPTON-UPON-SEVERN

'What the deuce has happened, man?' shouted Ravenscroft as he rushed into the police station in Upton.

'It's Stapleford, sir. He's escaped. There was nothing I could do, sir,' protested the hapless, red-faced, sweating policeman.

'What do you mean there was nothing you could do? When we left this station not three hours ago, Stapleford was locked up securely in the cells. Now you tell me you have lost him. How did this sorry state of affairs come about?' growled Ravenscroft.

'Well, sir, I went over to the Lion to get some refreshments for the prisoner and when I came back the cell door was open and he was gone,' replied the policeman looking down at his boots sorrowfully.

'Gone?' exclaimed Ravenscroft. 'How the blazes did that happen? Where were the keys?'

'They were in the drawer of the desk where they usually are kept, sir.'

'And it did not occur to you to take them with you when you went across to the Lion?'

'No, sir,' replied Hoskings, looking crestfallen.

'And I suppose you didn't think to lock the door of the police station behind you either?'

'I can't remember whether I did, or not, sir.'

'Hoskings, your days in this police force are swiftly coming to an end. Do I have to do everything in this station? What have you done about this man's escape?'

'Sent a telegram to Midwinter's, sir,'

'Yes, I know that. What have you done to apprehend the escaped prisoner?' continued an irritated Ravenscroft.

'I went to all the inns and stables in the town and asked them to contact us should a man of Stapleford's description try and secure a horse. Then I summoned a few of the local men and sent them to mount guard on the bridge and along the other two roads leading out of the town, should he try and make an escape that way, sir.'

'Well, at least that is something, although I suspect that you are too late. Stapleford could be halfway to Worcester or Evesham by now.'

'Must have been that man Parsons, sir, that old manservant of his,' suggested Crabb. 'He must have come in and let his master out.'

'Maybe, but I don't think Parsons was with Stapleford when he was arrested,' replied Ravenscroft. 'No, it must have been someone else. Stapleford must have been released by someone in this town, in which case that person is probably hiding him.'

'Shall I organize a house search?' suggested Hoskings.

'We only have ourselves available to do that. It would take far too long. Now who would be sheltering Stapleford?'

'Those Thexton brothers seem most likely, sir,' suggested Crabb.

'Yes, we know they have been in Stapleford's pay in the past. Well done, Tom. Come along, you as well, Hoskings. There is not a moment to lose if we are to recapture our prisoner.'

Ravenscroft rushed out of the door and along the streets of the town, closely followed by his two constables.

'The outer door of the yard is open,' said Crabb, as they drew near to the undertakers' premises.

'Check in the stables, Hoskings, and see if the horses are still there,' instructed Ravenscroft, banging his fist loudly on the door. 'There appears to be no one here. Put your shoulder against it, Crabb.'

Crabb ran at the door and, as it sprang open, the two men quickly entered the cold miserable room which Ravenscroft remembered from his first visit.

'There appears to be no one here, sir,' remarked Crabb.

'Try the inner room where they keep the coffins,' said Ravenscroft.

'There is no one there either, sir.'

'We will search upstairs. They could have hidden Stapleford up there,' said Ravenscroft, mounting the steps two at a time.

The detectives searched each of the three rooms where the three brothers slept before returning to the downstairs.

'Well, he does not appear to be here,' said Crabb.

Ravenscroft entered the claustrophobic, damp, dimly lit inner room, and looked around at its untidy contents. 'The coffin, Tom!' he suddenly exclaimed pointing to a large box which stood near the table in the centre of the room. 'Give me a hand to lift the lid.'

A reluctant Crabb aided Ravenscroft in his task.

'Oh my God!' exclaimed Crabb, as the two men peered into the coffin. 'Who on earth is that?'

'If I am not mistaken it appears to be an elderly woman who has recently died,' said Ravenscroft, looking down at the corpse.

'There is a name on the lid,' said Crabb. 'Margaret Johnston.'

'The horses and the hearse have gone, sir,' said a breathless Hoskings, entering the room. 'Oh my word, what is that?'

'Take yourself out of here, Hoskings, before you faint,' instructed Ravenscroft. 'Here, Crabb, put the lid back on and let the old woman rest in peace.'

'You think they are helping Stapleford escape by putting him in one of their coffins?' asked Crabb, once the three men had stepped out into the daylight.

'That may well be the case. It would be a good way to get him out of the town without being seen. Quickly, to the burial ground!'

The three men ran along several streets of the town before the old burial ground came into view.

'There is the hearse outside the church,' said Ravenscroft.

'There seems to be a funeral service going on,' said Crabb.

'We must halt proceedings,' said Ravenscroft, as they entered the churchyard and walked briskly over to where a group of mourners were standing before an open grave.

'. . . ashes to ashes, dust to dust . . .' intoned the clergyman.

'Stop!' shouted Ravenscroft, recognizing the three black-suited undertakers standing around the sides of the open grave. 'This service must cease!'

'What on earth!' exclaimed the clergyman looking up from his prayer book. 'Who are you?'

'I am Detective Inspector Ravenscroft of the local constabulary, and I have good reason to think that this burial is not all it seems,' continued Ravenscroft, noting that the Thexton brothers were looking at one another with apprehensive looks on their faces. 'May I ask who is being buried here today?'

'My mother, Mrs Johnston,' replied one of the mourners stepping forward.

'Did your mother possess a red patterned paisley shawl?' asked Ravenscroft.

'Yes, but I don't understand,' said the man.

'I am afraid have to tell you, my dear sir, that I have just seen such a shawl draped around the shoulders of your mother, inside a coffin at the premises of Shortcross and Maudlin,' continued Ravenscroft, as a loud gasp went up from several members of the congregation. 'Whoever is in this coffin, it is not your mother.'

'I don't understand,' protested the man.

'This is quite out of order—' stuttered the clergyman, at a loss for words.

'Mr Ravenscroft, this is all most irregular,' protested Reuben Thexton, drawing himself up to his full height and glaring at the detective.

'He's talking nonsense,' said Benjamin Thexton, appealing for support from the assembled mourners.

'Absolute nonsense!' added Simeon Thexton.

'I demand that you bring this coffin back to the surface,' said Ravenscroft ignoring the protestations of the three undertakers.

'My dear sir, we can't possibly do that,' interceded the perplexed clergyman. 'I have just performed the burial service.'

'And I have just informed you that the corpse within this coffin is not that of Mrs Johnston. I insist that it is brought back to the surface right away and that it is reopened,' demanded Ravenscroft. 'I have reason to believe there is a wanted man inside.'

'The man's mad!' protested Reuben, shaking his head from side to side.

'This is against the law of God!' proclaimed Benjamin as his brother Simeon moved away from the grave nervously.

'Open the coffin, I say!' shouted a voice from the back of the mourners, a cry that was taken up by other members of the crowd.

'We want to see who is inside,' demanded another mourner.

'I command you men to bring that coffin back,' protested Ravenscroft.

The three undertakers said nothing as they looked at each other, apprehensively.

'Damn it! If no one will assist us, then we must do it ourselves. Crabb, Hoskings, give me a hand to haul up this coffin,' said Ravenscroft suddenly jumping into the grave and securing the ropes around the box. 'The rest of you, take hold of those men and see that they do not escape.'

The angry crowd converged on the three undertakers, who quickly found themselves surrounded, as the policemen slowly lifted the coffin up and onto the surface of the ground.

'Now, Mr Thexton, will you remove the lid, or will I?' said Ravenscroft turning to face Reuben, as he brushed off the earth from his clothes.

'Open the coffin,' went up the cry again from several quarters.

'Aye, we want to see who is inside,' said an inquisitive young boy who had just wandered into the churchyard, and who was anxious not to be left out of the proceedings.

'Right, Crabb, Hoskings, put the handcuffs on those three men. Search their pockets for something useful to use to unscrew this coffin.'

'Here, sir,' said Crabb, handing over the tool which he had just recovered from Reuben Thexton's coat pocket.

Ravenscroft knelt down and removed the screws one by one. 'Now let us see what we have here.'

As the crowd surged forward, Ravenscroft slowly lifted the lid.

Someone at the back of the throng let out a high-pitched scream.

'It's Stapleford!' exclaimed Crabb. 'He's dead!'

'And if I am not mistaken, someone has strangled him!'

* * *

'Sit down, Mr Thexton,' said Ravenscroft, addressing Reuben Thexton across the table at the police station later that afternoon.

The undertaker said nothing as he sat down, and had his handcuffs removed by Constable Crabb.

'So, Mr Thexton, this is a dreadful situation which you have got yourself into — helping a prisoner to escape from custody; substitution of a dead body; murder by strangulation. Would you like to say anything in your defence before you and your brothers are transferred to the cells in Worcester, where you will all stand trial?' asked Ravenscroft, leaning across the table and seeking to make eye contact with his mournful suspect.

'I know nothing of Stapleford's death,' replied Reuben, throwing his head back and giving Ravenscroft a look of indifference.

'Oh, come now, Mr Thexton, we know you sprang Stapleford from the cells here when Constable Hoskings was visiting the Lion. You then took the doctor back to your premises where you strangled the man. We have the evidence that will convict you all. Why did you do that? Were you afraid that if we interrogated Stapleford further he would tell us all that we wanted to know about your business, how you removed fresh bodies from the churchyard and then sold them for monetary gain? Or did you never bury the bodies in the first place but delivered them directly to Stapleford? You might as well tell me the truth, sooner rather than later. You have been caught red-handed and you have nowhere else to go,' said Ravenscroft confidently.

Thexton stared at him for some seconds before speaking. 'All right, I admit it. Doctor Stapleford was an unscrupulous man. We helped him secure one corpse; he said it was for medical research, but then he demanded that we supply him with more bodies, and when we refused he threatened to expose us all to the authorities. There was nothing we could do but comply with his requests. We did not want to take poor Miss Cleaves to his house that night. We realized what he would do. Then, when we knew you had arrested him, we were frightened that he would tell you everything. When you and your constable left the station we saw it as our opportunity to release him from custody. We knew then that we would have to be rid of him for good. We couldn't take the chance that he would be arrested again, and that he would tell you everything.'

'And so you murdered Stapleford and substituted his body for that of Mrs Johnston?' said Ravenscroft, relieved that the truth was coming out at last.

'Yes, but we would have returned to the graveyard later tonight and buried the good lady on top of Stapleford's coffin,'

'That would have been very convenient,' said Ravenscroft, a note of cynicism in his voice. 'And which one of you strangled him?'

'Oh that was me. My brothers had nothing to do with it, I can assure you. They were out of the room preparing the horses for the funeral, so I was able to make the substitution. They are entirely innocent. I know I will hang,' answered the undertaker seemingly unconcerned by the plight he found himself in.

'I think that is almost certain. Now what can you tell me about the dead man found by the river? Did you know that he was not Simon Cleaves?' asked Ravenscroft.

'I knew nothing about the young man until we were instructed to collect his body and arrange for the burial,' replied Reuben earnestly.

'And Miss Cleaves — had you ever met her before the funeral? Have you ever visited Mathon Manor?'

'No, I knew nothing of the young lady, and only visited the house the day we collected her body.'

Ravenscroft studied his suspect for a few moments before turning to Crabb and giving instructions that he was to be taken back to the cells. He had not expected that Reuben Thexton would have admitted his crimes so easily, but it worried him that he might have been so forthcoming with his confession merely as an attempt to exonerate his brothers.

Crabb returned a few moments later with the second brother, Benjamin.

'Take a seat, Mr Thexton. Now then, what have you got to say about this ghastly business?'

The undertaker remained silent, staring over Ravenscroft's shoulder towards the small window at the top of the wall.

'We know that you and your two brothers have been supplying bodies to Dr Stapleford for quite some time, so there is no use denying that. We also know that it was you and your brothers who delivered Miss Cleaves's body to his house that night, despite the false alibi that your friends in the Plough provided for you. It must have been worrying for you when you saw that we had Stapleford in custody You took advantage of my constable's temporary absence from the station to spring him free from the cells. Your brother has admitted that it was he who strangled Stapleford.'

'That is not true. It was me who strangled him,' replied Benjamin staring directly at Ravenscroft.

'Go on.'

'When we returned to our premises we knew that we could not let Stapleford go, as he stood to implicate us all. Reuben wanted to drug him and then drown him in the Severn, but we decided that this would be too risky. Then Simeon suggested that if we killed him we could then bury him in place of Mrs Johnston. No one would be any the wiser and we would be free of Stapleford for ever. The only question that remained was who was to kill him. So we drew lots, and it fell to me to do the deed. That is all I have to say.'

'That is not what your brother has told us. He said that he strangled Stapleford while you and Simeon were seeing to the horses,' said Ravenscroft.

'My brother is merely seeking to protect me. Reuben did not kill Stapleford. I would not see him go to the gallows for something which he did not commit.'

'I see. Now, Mr Thexton, what do you know of the death of Mr Simon Cleaves? Was it you, or your brother who drowned the unfortunate man in the pond by the folly?'

'I am afraid I do not know what you are talking about. Neither I, nor my brothers, have ever had any contact with that gentleman. Why would we want to kill someone whom we did not even know?'

'Perhaps one of you could have been Anne Cleaves's lover? When did you meet the lady?'

'I know nothing about Miss Cleaves. The first time we met the young lady was at the burial service.'

'I don't suppose you ever met the schoolmaster, John Smith, before you attempted to bury him?'

'That is indeed so, Inspector,' answered Benjamin without concern.

'Right, you can go for now. I have to say I am not satisfied with your answers. Take him back to the cells, Crabb,' instructed Ravenscroft.

'You must believe me, Inspector, when I tell you that my brother is innocent. I seek only to admit my actions in strangling Stapleford, and all I seek now is to atone for my sins before I meet my Maker,' said Benjamin, as Crabb put the handcuffs on his outstretched wrists.

'Take him back to the cells,' repeated Ravenscroft, not looking up from his papers on the desk. He had found the pious sanctimonious utterings of the undertaker more than he could bear, and had not expected that Benjamin would have exonerated his brothers while implicating himself.

A few moments later Crabb returned to the room leading a handcuffed Simeon Thexton.

'You have spoken to my brothers? What have they told you?' asked the undertaker anxiously.

'Never mind what they have told me, Mr Thexton, I want to hear your side of this story,' said Ravenscroft, leaning back in his chair and staring directly at his suspect.

'It was a terrible thing which we have done. I know that. May God forgive us all,' replied Simeon, tears beginning to well up in his eyes.

'Then perhaps you could start by confessing your sins to me,' urged Ravenscroft. 'Whose idea was it to supply Dr Stapleford with recently deceased bodies?'

'That was entirely my own idea. Reuben and Benjamin were against it, but Stapleford offered us good money, and I eventually persuaded them to carry out the work,' said Simeon, bringing a handkerchief to his eyes.

'Sally Owens? How did you acquire her corpse?'

'Yes. We saw that the other undertakers had buried her, so the following night we returned to the burial ground, and we recovered her body from her coffin and delivered it to Stapleford. Will God ever forgive me?'

'I doubt it, Mr Thexton, and I know that twelve good men and true probably won't either. And Oliver Thompson, did you recover his body as well?' asked Ravenscroft.

'Yes, yes,' sobbed Simeon.

'And how many other bodies were there?'

'Three. May the good Lord save us! '

'Come, Thexton, enough of this melodramatic performance. It won't do you any good in the long run. Any jury will see through such religious humbug. Just answer the questions. Why did you decide to kill Stapleford?'

'When we took him back to our premises, he demanded that we help him escape from the town. He knew that everyone would be looking out for him. As he had no money he shouted that he wanted some of the money back that he had paid us, or he would go to the authorities and tell them everything. He was such an evil man. He wanted us to smuggle him out of the town in one of the coffins, and then let him have one of the horses to make his escape, but we knew we could not permit him to do that. We had to silence him,' sobbed Simeon, before blowing his nose loudly and then attempting to dry his eyes.

'Go on,' urged Ravenscroft after a moment's silence had elapsed.

'Well, that is all I can tell you.'

'I don't think so. I want to know which one of you strangled him?' asked Ravenscroft, half expecting the answer that he knew would be forthcoming.

'Reuben and Benjamin went out to the stables to prepare the horses, and I knew then that the escape plan would not work. Stapleford would not have travelled very far before you would have caught up with him, then everything would have come out, and so I crept up behind him and strangled him,' admitted Simeon.

'What did you use?' asked Ravenscroft.

'I am sorry, I don't understand,' replied the undertaker, puzzled.

'I want to know what you used to strangle him.'

'Oh, there was some rope nearby. I looped it around his neck and pulled it tight.'

'That is very interesting, Mr Thexton. You might be interested to know that your two brothers have each individually confessed to the same crime.'

'No, no, you must be mistaken. Neither Reuben nor Benjamin would do such a thing. No, it was me who killed that man. I did it to save us all, you must see that,' pleaded Simeon.

'This is all very neat,' said Ravenscroft throwing down his pencil on the table in frustration. 'When did you each decide to confess to Stapleford's murder?'

'I don't know what my brothers have told you. They have obviously lied to protect me. I am the youngest brother, as I am sure you are aware, and Benjamin and Reuben have always felt protective towards me, but whatever they have told you must be a lie. I killed that Stapleford, and I alone. They had nothing to do with it.'

'This is all quite unacceptable. Have you ever been to Glenforest School?' said Ravenscroft, deciding to change the direction of his questioning.

'No. I don't even know where this school is.'

'Did you kill John Smith, the schoolmaster?'

'No.'

'Did any of your brothers kill him?' asked Ravenscroft quickly.

'No.'

'What about Simon Cleaves? Were you Anne Cleaves's lover and did you drown her brother in the pond near the Folly?'

'No. No.'

'And did you then murder Anne Cleaves in her bedroom?'

'No. No.'

'What did you use to strangle her with?'

'No. No. Please stop!' cried out the undertaker, burying his head in his hands.

'Well!' shouted Ravenscroft, banging his fist down hard on the table.

'No! I had nothing to do with any of this,' pleaded Simeon.

'And what about your brothers: did any of them strangle Miss Cleaves or drown Simon Cleaves?'

'No, Reuben is a kind man. He would never do such a thing.'

'And your brother Benjamin — what about him?'

'Benjamin is such a gentle man. He could never hurt anyone. Will God not come to our aid? We have sinned, Lord, and we beg Your forgiveness for we have been sinners. Save us, Lord!' said Simeon, clasping his hands together and looking upwards as if in prayer.

'For goodness sake!' cried out Ravenscroft. 'I've had enough of all this nonsense. Take him back to the cells.'

'Come with me. Thexton,' said Crabb reapplying the handcuffs.

Ravenscroft watched as Crabb escorted the prisoner from the room, then stood up from the table and began pacing the floor. Each of his suspects had confessed to the crime of death by strangulation, and each brother had told a different story as they had sought to protect the other two. At first sight this appeared to be somewhat of a noble gesture, but Ravenscroft had come to the realization that this deception had been well thought out and planned beforehand. As each man had failed to implicate any one of the other two, it would be difficult for a jury to decide as to which had in fact committed the crime.

'Those three are as slippery as a bag of Severn eels,' said Crabb coming back into the room.

'I was expecting that they would each deny the accusation of murder; I had not expected that each would confess to the deed!' exclaimed Ravenscroft.

'You think they had anything to do with the other three murders?'

'Strangely enough I believed them when they professed not to know anything about the murders of Simon Cleaves and John Smith, and I cannot see that any of the three brothers could have been either the lover, or murderer, of Anne Cleaves. However, we must make sure that they all go down for body snatching, and then leave it to the lawyers to decide as to which one of them actually strangled Stapleford.'

'They could all have had a hand it,' suggested Crabb.

'I am sure you are correct, Tom, but it will be devil of a job to prove it. At least we are rid of that dreadful Stapleford, and I suppose it is rather ironic that a man who spent so much of his time recovering corpses from coffins should finally end up in one himself.'

'That does mean that if Stapleford was our murderer, we will never know the truth.'

'I don't really believe that Stapleford was our man, do you, Tom?'

'No, I suppose not.'

'Which leaves us with either Gervase Webster, Marcus Choke, or Horace Smeaton as our killer. I am inclined to rule out Smeaton, which leaves Webster or Choke — unless there is someone else that we have missed. Of course, how could we have been so blind! We have been completely taken in! It was all to do with that letter which sent us to Ludlow! We have been so stupid to have overlooked that. The answer to this mystery has been there in front of us for all this time!' exclaimed Ravenscroft.

'What do you mean, sir?' asked Crabb, bewildered.

Ravenscroft's deliberations were suddenly interrupted by a loud tap on the door.

'Come in.'

'Excuse me, sir,' said Hoskings entering the room. 'But these have just come for you.'

'Thank you,' said Ravenscroft eagerly accepting the two envelopes.

'This must be the reply to the enquiry regarding Anne Cleaves's will which we sent to Gervase Webster at Mathon Manor, and the other one looks like a reply to my telegram sent to the Criminal Records Office at the Yard. Let us hope that one or more of these will confirm my suspicions,' said Ravenscroft, tearing open the envelopes.

'What do they say?' asked Crabb, eagerly.

'It is just as I thought: Anne Cleaves named her cousin Gervase Webster as the chief beneficiary of her will. He stands to inherit Mathon Manor on her death, unless she married first,' said Ravenscroft reading the first paper. 'But then there are apparently a number of other legacies. Good Lord!'

'What is it, sir?' asked Crabb, as Ravenscroft tore open the other envelope.

'This confirms everything, Tom. Prepare the trap. We have an arrest to make!'

CHAPTER TWELVE

GLENFOREST

Ravenscroft strode up to the front door of Glenforest Preparatory School and grasped the bell pull vigorously, knowing that the next few minutes would confirm, or disprove, all of his suspicions, and hopefully lead to the arrest that he had long been seeking.

'Yes, sir,' said a young boy, opening the door.

'We have called to see Mr Smeaton,' answered Ravenscroft, half expecting that the door would have been opened by the headmaster.

'He's in his study,' answered the boy with casual indifference, before turning away.

Ravenscroft and Crabb stepped into the hallway and quickly walked along the corridor until they reached the open door of Smeaton's study.

'Inspector Ravenscroft,' said the headmaster, looking up from his desk, where he had been studying a large ledger, with Choke at his side.

'Mr Smeaton. Mr Choke,' said Ravenscroft. 'It is good that I find you both here. I have some more urgent questions for you both.'

'Well, yes, I suppose you have,' replied a perplexed Smeaton staring at the detective through his glasses.

'I will go, Headmaster,' said Choke about to take his leave.

'I would be obliged if you would remain, Mr Choke, as this matter concerns both of you gentlemen,' said Ravenscroft.

Choke nodded as Ravenscroft continued, 'On the morning of Smith's funeral you handed us a letter, Mr Choke, which had apparently been delivered here in that morning's post.'

'Yes, that is correct,' confirmed Choke.

'This letter, purporting to have been written by a young lady called Rosemary by name, and written from the Feathers Hotel in Ludlow, was addressed to John Smith, urging him to come to that town as soon as possible. My colleague, Constable Crabb and I travelled by train that afternoon to Ludlow, but our attempts to find this elusive lady came to nought. On reflection this was hardly surprising as I have now come to the conclusion that this "Rosemary" does not in fact exist. She was obviously the fictitious creation of the person who wrote the letter.'

'How extraordinary,' uttered Smeaton.

'I believe that the main purpose of the letter was to ensure that we were sent on this fruitless adventure to Ludlow, so that its author would be able to visit Anne Cleaves in her bedroom at Mathon Manor, where he was then able to commit this atrocity undetected. The killer knew that we were about to return to Mathon that same afternoon to question Anne Cleaves further, and that she would in all probability have confessed to the crime of her brother's death, thereby implicating him also in the murder. He knew that she would have to be silenced in order to prevent that happening.'

'This is all quite fascinating, but I do not see how all this concerns either myself or Mr Choke,' said Smeaton, after Ravenscroft had paused in his narrative to allow his words to be take effect.

'Before visiting here today, I paid a visit to the local post office in Bromyard. The postmaster checked his records, and was able to confirm that no letters were delivered to this school on the day in question.'

'I do not understand where all this getting us,' said Smeaton rubbing his forehead.

'From all of this, we can now conclude that the letter was either written by someone here at the school, or that it was delivered by hand. Its main purpose, as I have just stated, was to prevent us from interviewing Miss Cleaves, and in that objective it was highly successful. Mr Choke, when we spoke to you last you mentioned that during Miss Cleaves's visits to the school she had shown a great interest in the work of the Church Missionary Society.'

'That was indeed so,' replied Choke.

'And that it was your ambition that one day you might have sufficient funds to travel to Sierra Leone in order to establish a school there?'

'Yes.'

'Choke, this is the first I have heard of this,' interjected Smeaton.

'It was just a dream I had, Headmaster; nothing has been arranged, I can assure you,' replied Choke, attempting to placate his superior.

'You might be interested to know, Mr Choke, that I have today received a summary of Miss Cleaves's will, in which she leaves you the sum of two thousand pounds and, I quote, "to further your Christian endeavours in Sierra Leone."'

'Thank the Lord. So she did not forget,' replied Choke attempting to hold back the tears, and clasping his hands together. 'The good lady; she remembered!'

'Two thousand pounds!' echoed a startled Smeaton.

'It would appear so. You and your cause, Mr Choke, obviously made quite an impression on the lady. However, I am afraid that I am also the bringer of bad news. As we now know that Simon Cleaves was killed before he attained the age of twenty-five years, all the estate of Mathon Manor and its possessions, under the terms of his late father's will, are to be sold, and the proceeds bequeathed to the Foundling Hospital in London.'

'How very commendable,' uttered Smeaton.

'Consequently Anne Cleaves stood to inherit little, except a small annuity, under the terms of this, her late father's will. In the light of Simon Cleaves's death before the age of twenty-five, her will is now of little value. So, I am afraid, Mr Choke, although Anne Cleaves's intention was entirely honourable, events have since made it largely invalid. Of course, the will was made some weeks ago before her brother was murdered, and I have no doubt that if his body had never been recovered the terms of Miss Cleaves's will would then have come into force.'

'I see,' said a crestfallen Choke, his eyes full of tears. 'The money is not important: Miss Cleaves's intentions were entirely honourable. I will treasure her name for ever more.'

'What an extraordinary turn of events,' said Smeaton.

'Indeed. I have today also received a telegram from a former colleague of mine at the Criminal Records Office in London. I asked him to check their records to see if anyone in this case has been involved in any criminal activity in the past. Shall I go on, Mr Choke?'

'Choke, what is this?' asked Smeaton, as Ravenscroft observed that the colour had suddenly drained from the young teacher's face.

'It was all such a long time ago,' muttered Choke, turning towards the window so that his face could not be observed by the two policemen.

'Eight years ago to be precise. The record states that one Marcus Choke was convicted at the Old Bailey on a charge of embezzlement of funds. Would you like to enlighten us further, Mr Choke?' asked Ravenscroft confidently.

'When I left school I was engaged as a junior clerk in a firm of solicitors in London. Some monies paid by a client went missing, and the finger of suspicion was pointed at me. The firm had little evidence of my supposed wrongdoing, but I was nevertheless sentenced to six years' imprisonment.

It was only later, three years later to be precise, that new evidence came to light. Another clerk in the practice had repeated the same crime and, when arrested, had confessed to the earlier offence. I was then released,' narrated a mournful Choke, still looking out of the window.

'Why didn't you tell me all this when we engaged you to teach here two years ago?' asked a startled Smeaton.

'I saw no reason. I had been proven innocent of the crime. What good would it have served to admit this false stain on my character?' pleaded Choke turning round to face his employer, who merely shook his head and said nothing.

'With all due respect, Mr Choke, there is no reference on the record that states that you were eventually cleared of the crime,' said Ravenscroft. 'I am sure that had that been the case your guilty record would have been removed from files.'

'Then your information must be incorrect,' said Choke. 'Headmaster, I was totally innocent of that crime. You must believe me.'

'I can assure you that our records are quite correct, Mr Choke. I believe that you committed this crime of embezzlement, and that you served your full time in prison before being released. You then sought employment here, in a school that was so far away from London, in a remote area of the country, that no one would ever recognize you. But then one day, approximately six months ago, another young man by the name of John Smith arrived at Glenforest. I doubt whether this was his real name; perhaps he had been a former prisoner in the same institution where you had been imprisoned? If so, that must have posed difficulties for you. Did he blackmail you, threaten to expose you, or was he just as anxious to keep his past hidden as well? Either way, you must have lived in fear that one day Smith would tell your employer everything about your dark past.'

'This is all nonsense. I have told you I was set free when another man finally confessed to the crime; as for Smith, I had never set eyes on him before,' replied Choke anxiously.

'For two years you had sought to forget your past as you taught the young minds at Glenforest. Then a beautiful young lady arrives one day. You talk together. She expresses an interest in your plan to help the poor and ignorant natives of Sierra Leone, so much so that she travels to London and makes a will that will provide you with the required funds in the event of her own death, but then interest and concern turned to love and affection. You met in secret. You became lovers. You wrote her letters. Her brother learned of her love for you, and strongly disapproved of the match,' continued Ravenscroft, realizing that he had at last cornered his quarry.

'Stop, stop! This is all fabrication. I liked Miss Cleaves, I admit that, but I was never her lover,' protested Choke.

'I believe that you and Anne Cleaves decided to elope together, but that Simon Cleaves followed you that day to the Folly where he confronted you both,' continued Ravenscroft. 'Did you deliberately murder Simon Cleaves, or did he die as the result of an accident? Which was it, Mr Choke?'

'Neither. I was not there. I did not kill Simon Cleaves,' answered a desperate Choke shaking his head.

'You then weighted down his pockets with stones and rocks so that the body would sink to the bottom of the pond, but then you both realized that as he had died before inheriting the estate, it would have to look as though Simon Cleaves was still alive, at least for another two weeks, or you would both stand to lose everything. So Anne invented the fabrication that her brother had left home that same day, without word of his intentions. Then you both realized that Simon Cleaves would have to make one final appearance, after his twenty-fifth birthday, so that the inheritance would then pass to Anne Cleaves, and not to the Foundling orphans. That was where John Smith came into the plan. I believe you lured him away from the school that night, perhaps under some pretext that he had been recognized as the former criminal he was and, once out of sight, you brutally struck him on the head. You had also neatly disposed of the one person who could have exposed your former criminal past. All that now remained of the plan was to plant the body by the side of the river in Upton, with certain former possessions of Simon Cleaves in his pockets, to indicate that he was indeed the landowner. Smith would have been buried, but everyone would have concluded that it was Simon Cleaves who was in that grave. Anne would then have inherited the estate, and you, Mr Choke, would no doubt have married her at some later date and become the new owner of Mathon Manor. It was a very ingenious plan carefully arranged down to the last detail, from the far off town where no one would recognize the corpse, to the careful planting of Simon Cleaves's old horse nearby, which you had no doubt kept out of sight until that fateful day to Anne, insisting on a quick funeral before suspicions could be aroused. All this may well have worked, except for Lady Cleaves who mistakenly thought she had heard mysterious sounds coming from inside the coffin at the funeral service. Then, as things began to unravel, and we questioned Miss Cleaves, you knew it would only be a matter of time before she told us everything. You then wrote her a desperate letter instructing her to leave the window of the storeroom open so that you could meet her in her room, at the same time making sure that we had gone on a false errand to Ludlow.'

'No! No!' cried out Choke, clasping his ears tightly with his hands. 'Stop! Stop! This is all wrong!'

'After strangling your lover, you recovered the incriminating letters and made your escape through the woods. Where are those letters now, Choke?'

'What letters? I know nothing of any letters. This is all a terrible mistake,' cried out a frantic Choke.

'Have you destroyed them, or have you hidden them somewhere?'

'No!'

'We will find them, Choke, I promise you that. Why don't you admit everything?'

'I keep telling you, I did not commit any of this.'

'It will be much better for you if you confess your crimes,' urged Ravenscroft.

'This is all a terrible mistake,' cried the schoolmaster looking intently at the policemen before turning towards Smeaton. 'You believe me, do you not, Headmaster? You cannot believe that I am capable of such evil deeds.'

'I . . . I . . .' stuttered Smeaton, seeking to distance himself from the helpless teacher by moving away from the desk.

'It is all over, Choke,' said Ravenscroft with an air of finality.

'No, no. You have got all this wrong. May God help me!' cried out Choke.

'Marcus Choke, I am about to say something to you, and after I have said it, if you reply, be very careful what you say in response, because what you say may be given in evidence against you,' said Ravenscroft with solemnity.

'No! No!' cried out the helpless schoolmaster sinking onto his knees and covering his head with his arms and hands.

'Marcus Choke, you are to be taken into custody on suspicion of having caused the deaths of John Smith, Simon Cleaves and Anne Cleaves during the month of March 1891,' continued Ravenscroft.

'No, I tell you that you have the wrong man!' sobbed Choke, as he collapsed in a heap on the floor.

CHAPTER THIRTEEN

WORCESTER, THREE WEEKS LATER

As Ravenscroft made his way past the imposing statue of Queen Victoria and up the steps that lead into the interior of the Worcester Shire hall, his thoughts turned once again to the events of the previous few days.

Choke had been brought to trial charged with the murders of Simon Cleaves, Anne Cleaves and the teacher John Smith. The prosecution had engaged the services of a leading Birmingham lawyer, although Gervase Webster had suggested that they might have considered engaging the expertise of the famous advocate Sefton Rawlinson, but apparently the great man had been struck down by a particularly nasty bout of gout and had therefore reluctantly declined the invitation. Ravenscroft himself had given evidence the day before, and the seats inside the building had been fully occupied for each day of the trial, as the case had been widely reported by both the local and national newspapers. Choke had not been able to afford the costs of any lawyer of note, but that role had been ably filled by Timothy Muncaster, who had eagerly volunteered his services, seeing it as an excellent opportunity to at last establish his name in the legal profession.

Muncaster had risen to the occasion with both energy and high theatrical endeavour, and although everyone had regarded his cause as lost, he had strenuously argued that there had been no evidence to indicate that his client had actually been in the vicinity of the Folly on the morning of the murder of Simon Cleaves, and that in any case the victim had probably met his death as the result of an accident. He had then gone on to claim that no one had actually seen his client enter Mathon Manor on the day of Anne Cleaves's death, and that likewise there had been no witnesses to the placement of the schoolmaster's body in the field at Upton. But then the prosecution had made great play of the letter which had prevented Ravenscroft and Crabb from interviewing Anne Cleaves on the day of her death, and the fact that Choke had persuaded the dead woman to leave him a substantial sum of money in her will had done little to aid his cause. There had also been the disclosure of Choke's criminal past and how he had falsely claimed to have been innocent of that former crime. The damning piece of evidence against him though had been the discovery, two days after his arrest, of one of Anne Cleaves's letters, addressed to her lover, which had been found by Crabb secreted behind the back of the mirror in Choke's bedroom at Glenforest. After that revelation, it was fortunate for the defence that Muncaster had not been compelled to call his client to the stand.

Now that both sides had presented all their evidence, and had cross-examined the many witnesses, there had been the summing up by both barristers, and again Muncaster had risen fully to the occasion, presenting his client as a deeply religious, caring man, who had sought only to serve others; a portrait which had been torn to shreds by the prosecution who had preferred to depict the man on trial as an evil monster who had slaughtered three innocent people and who had shown little remorse or principle for his actions.

Ravenscroft entered the packed courtroom, and was directed to his seat by a gesturing Crabb. Now it was the turn of the judge to commence his summing up of the case.

'Should be over by today,' whispered Crabb.

'Let us hope so. It won't be long before we are here again to testify against those Thextons,' replied Ravenscroft.

As the judge faced the jury and outlined the facts of the case before them, Ravenscroft looked around the court. In the dock sat the figure of Marcus Choke, his face strained, his shoulders slumped, a distant forlorn expression on his face, the portrait of a man who had long known that he was defeated, and who was now clearly resigned to his fate. The man appeared to be so alone and desolate in the world that Ravenscroft had almost begun to have some feelings of compassion for him, until he reminded himself that this was the man who had murdered three innocent people in ways that were almost incomprehensible and evil to understand.

Then below the dock was young Muncaster, clearly relishing the importance of the occasion and yet appearing nervous and somewhat restless, no doubt wondering whether he had done all he could have done to save his client, and apprehensive as to what the outcome of the case might yet be,

In the row behind the barristers, sat the upright, black-veiled figure of Lady Cleaves, her face covered so that it would conceal any kind of emotion that might be expressed there, that might be seen by some as a possible sign of weakness. Next to her the immaculately dressed Gervase Webster taking a keen interest in all that was taking place, and no doubt believing that he could have made a better argument for the prosecution had not his personal involvement in the case prevented him from doing so.

In a row towards the back of the courtroom, Ravenscroft noticed the servants of Mathon Lodge with Mansfield the butler at the end of their row, Charlotte, the maid, her eyes more wet than dry, and Mrs Wills looking anxious and worn, each now probably wondering what would happen to the great house and whether their roles would continue there. Next to them was the crumpled untidy figure of Horace Smeaton squinting into the dark interior of the court through his cloudy spectacles.

Further along the row, he noticed the small figure of Anthony Midwinter, who, although he had not attended the court on previous days, had obviously made the journey from Ledbury that day to witness the conclusion to the trial.

Ravenscroft's thoughts turned back to the many trials he had attended in his career, and of the many criminals he had brought to justice over the years, from the pickpockets, pimps and fraudsters of Whitechapel, to the petty crooks and murderers of the Three Counties, and how some of those cases had been easily won, while others had been lost with great difficulty, and how guilty men had walked free, as other more pitiful souls had been convicted of lesser crimes — and he wondered now whether he had done enough in this case to secure a conviction. The incriminating letter, the legacy of the will, the suspect's criminal past, his association with both the young woman and his former prison inmate, the opportunity to commit all of the crimes, all stood to go against the schoolmaster, and yet he knew that juries could be fickle and that all his good work could be undone in a few simple words.

Now the judge had finished addressing the jury, Choke had been taken back to his cells to await his fate, the barristers on both sides were exchanging pleasantries before disappearing from view, and the packed benches of the court were no less in numbers as their occupants seemed reluctant to relinquish them before the verdict was announced.

'You think they will be a long time, sir?' asked Crabb.

'I don't honestly know, Tom. All I can say is that from my experience the shorter the time spent in deliberation before arriving at a verdict usually means that the case is clear cut, whereas the longer time spent often means that issues of uncertainty have been raised and that the outcome is in doubt.'

'I think it is obvious to everyone that he did it.'

'You seem very confident, Tom.'

'Aren't you, sir?'

'Yes, I suppose so, but what if we are wrong, Tom; what if Choke did not commit these crimes; what if we have arrested the wrong man; does that thought not concern you?'

'Well, yes, sir, but I still think he did it,' replied Crabb.

'I wish I had your confidence,' smiled Ravenscroft. 'I suppose we have done our best, but something is of concern to me. Everything seemed to fall into place quite easily at the end — the Rosemary letter, Choke's criminal past, Anne Cleaves's legacy — that I have sometimes wondered whether all this has been too perfect. But take no notice of my indecision, Tom; waiting for the result of a jury's deliberations is always an anxious time, when one even begins to doubt one's own actions.'

'I thought Muncaster put up a good fight,' remarked Crabb, after a few minutes of silence had elapsed.

'Yes, this case will no doubt make his name, whatever the verdict,' answered Ravenscroft.

'What will happen to Mathon Manor now?'

'Well, as Simon Cleaves never attained his twenty-fifth birthday, then his father, old Martin Cleaves's will still stands, and everything will have to be sold.'

'The Foundling Hospital will benefit a great deal.'

'Yes, I have no doubt that many a young person will be given a good start in life, so at least some good will have come from all this.'

'Gervase Webster will be annoyed.'

'Oh, I think Mr Webster will have enough money put aside to see him in the comfort to which he has long been accustomed.'

'The jury must be coming back,' interrupted Crabb as the volume of noise in the crowded courtroom increased. 'They have arrived at their decision quickly.'

Ravenscroft said nothing as he watched the prosecution and defence lawyers returning to the court, closely followed by a dejected Choke who sank onto the bench within the dock. Now everyone was standing for the judge, after which the jury members began to file back into the room, one by one, to their places.

'Prisoner will stand.'

'Members of the jury have you agreed upon the verdict?' asked the clerk of the court.

A hush descended on the room, as people leaned forward in eager anticipation.

'We have,' replied the foreman of the jury.

'And what is your verdict? Do you find the prisoner guilty, or not guilty, of the murder of Simon Cleaves?' continued the clerk.

'Guilty!'

Loud cries of surprise filled the room.

'Silence in court!' shouted the judge above the noise, as he banged his wooden hammer down on the table before him.

'Do you find the prisoner guilty or not guilty of the murder of Anne Cleaves?' asked the clerk.

'Guilty!'

Again more cries filled the courtroom as the judge shouted, 'Silence in court,' above the noise.

'Do you find the prisoner guilty or not guilty of the murder of John Smith?' asked the clerk.

'Guilty!'

Choke slumped onto the bench and covered his face with his hands, but the warders on either side of him forced him back onto his feet.

Applause now broke out in certain sections of the courtroom. One or two people cheered.

All eyes now turned from the hapless prisoner towards the judge, who slowly placed the black square cloth on top of his wig.

'Marcus Choke, you have been found guilty of the murders of Simon Cleaves, Anne Cleaves and John Smith. This court doth ordain that you be taken from hence to the place whence you came, and from thence to the place of execution—'

'No! I am innocent. You have the wrong man!' shouted out Choke, desperately.

The judge ignored the plea, as he continued with his words of finality.

'Your honour, I wish to bring forth an urgent appeal,' said an anxious Muncaster springing to his feet and confronting the judge, before turning on his heels and waving his arm in the direction of the benches, as if seeking support for his cause. 'My client is entirely innocent of these crimes. The defence demands a retrial!'

'Mr Muncaster, this will not do!' said the judge, after angrily bringing down his gavel again. 'This is not the time or place for this as a man of your learning and education should know! Disgraceful! Take the prisoner down!'

A protesting Choke was dragged out of the dock and taken down the stairs, as the room was suddenly filled by loud chatter and cries as the benches began to empty.

'Well, sir, that's that,' remarked Crabb, standing up and noticing that Ravenscroft was sitting in silence. 'Is something wrong, sir?'

'It's all a question of Anne Cleaves's will, don't you see?' replied Ravenscroft suddenly springing to his feet. 'It has been about that all the time.'

'I don't understand you, sir,' said Crabb, baffled. 'I think Mr Midwinter is trying to attract our attention from the other side of the courtroom.'

'Quickly, Tom, I must have a word with Gervase Webster before he leaves,' said Ravenscroft, beginning to push his way through the chattering crowds.

'Mr Ravenscroft, I must have an urgent word with you,' cried out Midwinter as he neared the centre of the courtroom.

'Mr Midwinter,' acknowledged Ravenscroft, as he made his way across the crowded room. 'If you will excuse me for one minute, I must first have a word with Mr Webster.'

'I fear a grave injustice has been done. I have just seen the man who was at the graveside that day,' continued

Midwinter, but Ravenscroft had already reached the huddled group of barristers.

'Well done, Muncaster. You did your best. No one could have done better, but it was a difficult case,' said Gervase Webster, vigorously shaking Muncaster's hand, causing the young barrister to drop a handful of sheets on the floor.

'Mr Webster, a word if I may,' said Ravenscroft, quickly reaching down and retrieving the papers before Muncaster could do so. 'When Miss Cleaves visited your chambers in the Temple and told you that she wished to make a will, I presume that you were not able to assist her?'

'Yes, that was indeed so,' replied the barrister, a puzzled expression on his face.

'May I ask why?'

'When she told me that she intended making me the chief beneficiary, I told her that it would be unethical if I was to draw up the will in person,' answered Webster.

'So, what transpired next, Mr Webster?' continued Ravenscroft.

'Well, I recommended her to young Muncaster here.'

'That is the man!' shouted an agitated Midwinter, as he approached the group.

'I am sorry, I don't understand,' said Webster. 'What is all this about?'

'That is the man!' repeated Midwinter, pointing at Muncaster. 'That is the man I saw at the graveyard! It was only when he stood up a minute ago, to address the judge, that I realized he was the man.'

'I have no doubt of it, Mr Midwinter,' said Ravenscroft reaching into his pocket and taking out a sheet of folded paper. 'This is the letter that you, Muncaster, deposited at Glenforest School, purporting to have been written by the elusive "Rosemary". If I compare the handwriting on this letter with the handwriting on these sheets of paper which you have just dropped I am sure we shall see a number of close similarities.'

Muncaster said nothing as he glared at Ravenscroft.

'On the day I interviewed you in your chambers, Mr Webster, you overheard our conversation, Muncaster, and knew that we were about to arrest Miss Cleaves. You knew then that you would have to act quickly to silence her. I also have no doubt that you planted the incriminating love letter in your client's bedroom at Glenforest to cruelly implicate poor Mr Choke. It is all over with you, Muncaster.'

'Muncaster, is this true?' asked Gervase Webster.

'Damn you all!' yelled Muncaster, suddenly throwing his remaining papers into Ravenscroft's face before making a run for the door.

'Crabb!' shouted Ravenscroft.

'I have him, sir,' said Crabb securing the fugitive in a strong grip round his shoulders.

'Confound you all! I dashed nearly got away with it as well. Best say no more though. Might need it for my defence, I suppose,' said Muncaster. 'Bad luck though, and all that.'

POSTSCRIPT

Timothy Muncaster stood trial for the murders of Simon Cleaves, Anne Cleaves and John Smith. Although he conducted his own spirited defence and was acquitted on the charge of murdering Simon Cleaves, he was found guilty of the other two killings, and was hanged at Worcester gaol. It was rumoured that as he mounted the scaffold he insisted on warmly shaking hands with all those in attendance before giving a lengthy theatrical oration which ended with the final words uttered by Sydney Carton from Charles Dickens's *A Tale of Two Cities*.

Reuben Thexton was eventually found guilty of the murder of Stapleford, and met a similar fate, despite the confessions of his two brothers each claiming sole responsibility for the crime. Benjamin and Simeon Thexton received lengthy prison sentences for their roles in the 'resurrection of dead bodies', and were said to have both emigrated to Australia on their release, where they resumed their former occupations in the state of New South Wales.

Simon and Anne Cleaves were buried, side by side, next to their late parents in the small churchyard in the village of Mathon. Mathon Manor itself was sold and the proceeds given to the Foundling Hospital in London, where many young babies and children benefitted from the legacy and were given a good start in life.

Gervase Webster's career flourished. He took the leading prosecuting role in a number of prominent murder trials, and eventually became a high court judge, where he became famous for his methodical summing up of cases.

Master Richard Ravenscroft was not sent to Glenforest Preparatory School, which Horace Smeaton continued to administer for the next ten years before the premises were eventually sold. In the early twentieth century the buildings became a hospital for the sick and poor of Bromyard, although they were later converted into luxury apartments for the elderly.

Marcus Choke eventually fulfilled his dream of travelling to Sierra Leone, where he built a school for the young and needy children of that country. He became a much respected and learned figure in the community there as his school grew in size and importance. He called the establishment The Anne Cleaves Memorial School.

Anthony Midwinter continued to attend funerals . . .

THE END

ALSO BY KERRY TOMBS

INSPECTOR RAVENSCROFT DETECTIVE MYSTERIES

Book 1: THE MALVERN MURDERS
Book 2: THE WORCESTER WHISPERERS
Book 3: THE LEDBURY LAMPLIGHTERS
Book 4: THE TEWKESBURY TOMB
Book 5: THE DROITWICH DECEIVERS
Book 6: THE PERSHORE POISONERS
Book 7: THE UPTON UNDERTAKERS

FREE KINDLE BOOKS

Do you love mysteries, historical fiction and romance? Join 1,000s of readers enjoying great books through our mailing list. You'll get new releases and great deals every week from one of the UK's leading independent publishers.

Join today, and you'll get your first bargain book this month!

www.joffebooks.com

Follow us on Facebook, Twitter and Instagram @joffebooks

Thank you for reading this book. If you enjoyed it please leave feedback on Amazon, and if there is anything we missed or you have a question about then please get in touch. The author and publishing team appreciate your feedback and time reading this book.

We're very grateful to eagle-eyed readers who take the time to contact us. Please send any errors you find to corrections@joffebooks.com. We'll get them fixed ASAP.

Printed in Great Britain
by Amazon

62070888R00128